W9-CDH-670

MURDER IN EXILE

Vincent H. O'Neil

MURDER IN EXILE

THOMAS DUNNE BOOKS ✦ ST. MARTIN'S MINOTAUR
NEW YORK

THOMAS DUNNE BOOKS.
An imprint of St. Martin's Press.

www.minotaurbooks.com

Library of Congress Cataloging-in-Publication Data

O'Neil, Vincent H.
Murder in Exile / Vincent H. O'Neil
p. cm.
ISBN 0-312-35207-7
EAN 978-0-312-35207-3
1. Insurance adjusters—Fiction. [1. Florida—Fiction.] I. Title.
PS3615.N48M87 2006
813'.6—dc22
2005054756

First Edition: April 2006

10 9 8 7 6 5 4 3 2 1

For my mother and father

ACKNOWLEDGMENTS

I would like to thank everyone involved with the St. Martin's Press Malice Domestic Best First Traditional Mystery Contest, which this book won in 2005. I would also like to thank my editor, Ruth Cavin, and her assistant, Toni Plummer, for all their efforts in bringing my book to print.

MURDER IN EXILE

CHAPTER ONE

"So that's the whole idea. I come down here to sunny Florida, hang out for a while, do a little background checking for local lawyers, and make sure I keep my earnings below a certain level."

I reached across the concrete chessboard as I spoke. The board was inlaid into a small concrete table-and-chairs arrangement common to the seaside parks in my new home of Exile, Florida. Gray Toliver, a tanned and composed local retiree who played chess with me most Wednesday mornings, took in my words with obvious skepticism.

Gray was the closest friend I had made since blowing into town nine months earlier, and he was still the only one who had been told this story. I had been playing chess with him once or twice a week for six months, but until that day he had not asked very much about my background or why a thirty-year-old man was living the life of a beach bum.

"Okay, Frank." Gray took his eyes off me to move one of his pieces. He was a much better chess player than I was, but then again he'd been whipping the local talent for a decade before I got there. "Let me get this straight. You came down here to get away from your failed business up north—"

“ ‘Failed’ is a strong word.” I hadn’t meant to say that, but the sting from the memories was still sore. Luckily, the words had come out unheated. I liked Gray and wanted to keep him as a friend.

“Your business went belly-up. The Frank Cole Computer Company, or whatever you called it, went bankrupt. Right?” His voice was as even as mine, but this was one of the times that I didn’t like him quite so much. He’d been a Chief Petty Officer in the navy in a job involving some whiz-bang analysis of airplane wings. I could easily hear a generation of former swabbies telling bored children and uninterested wives just what a pain old Chief Toliver had been.

“Yes, Gray.”

“So, saying it failed is pretty accurate.”

A gull screeched overhead before it flew between two of the park’s trees. The surf, one hundred yards away, rumbled on in and then went back out as if it were inhaling and exhaling. I moved another chess piece without answering.

“And some psycho judge attached your future earnings as part of the bankruptcy. So out of spite you’ve resolved to live the life of a pauper.”

“Hopefully not an entire life. The judge was way out of bounds with that ruling and it’s certain to get overturned.”

“Spoken like a true denizen of death row.”

“Come again?” He’d moved while talking and seriously hurt my chances of winning this match. Well, truth is, I’d only managed to beat him twice in dozens of contests.

“I just wonder how many people go to the electric chair saying those same words. ‘The judge was out of bounds. The appeal will come through.’ I imagine some people spend a lifetime in prison saying those words.”

“Let’s hope it’s not a lifetime.” I pretended to stare at the board. In truth, there was a lot to recommend my spending the next fifty or so years in the Panhandle town of Exile. After three bruising years building up my company and three more losing it, I wasn't sure that I ever wanted any more responsibility than the simple fact-checking duties I had here in sunny Florida.

"One question. Bankruptcy is supposed to be a fresh start." Gray was amazingly well read and seemed to know a lot about everything. If he weren't so darned annoying when sharing his knowledge, he'd be on the cocktail party circuit instead of playing board games with guys like me. "So how do you end up with your future earnings attached, if it's supposed to be a clean slate?"

Gray had hit on one of the main flaws in the judge's ruling. Mark Ruben, formerly my college roommate and now a high-powered Manhattan attorney, maintained that an appeal held great promise because my case was the first one in which a judge had done something like this. When a business like mine is liquidated, almost all debt obligations are terminated one way or the other. The judge in my case had essentially written a new chapter into that law by attaching my future earnings as part of the settlement. Although Mark had been adamant that the law did not allow this kind of penalty, he had been equally sure that the judge was within his purview to set such a precedent.

Lawyers are like that. I had simply asked Mark if my wages above a certain level of income were in fact attached at that point regardless of a possible reversal. He'd nodded, and I had started getting used to the idea that I would be working off a titanic debt for the rest of my life.

"It was a combination of things. The judge in my case is dotty as all get-out. He should have been retired years ago, he was half asleep through the entire proceeding. Then there's a group in the legal community that wants this as a standard penalty in all corporate bankruptcies—"

"So they can get bigger awards."

"Yes. But you're right, this is supposed to be a fresh start."

"It's also supposed to get the debts off the books one way or another. Dragging these things out isn't going to be any good for the bookkeeping," Gray pointed out. As I said, Gray was a man of many parts.

"Anyway, one of the bigger corporate-fraud bankruptcies ended that very same week. A huge corporation. You might have heard about these guys: They cooked the books, bought girlfriends and condos using company money—"

"Bullitel. The telecommunications company?"

"You're an amazing guy, Gray. Yep, that's them." I watched Gray tear the game apart without seeming to look at the board. "The prosecution absolutely blew that case, and when it got tossed, there was a real uproar. Corporate fraud hit the front page again, and suddenly my judge thought he'd reverse the tide by nailing me to the floorboards."

Gray didn't announce the checkmate when he made the move. We both sat there for a moment, as if appreciating the climbing sun and the sounds of the beach. I finally stood up, actually having some place to go for once.

"Off to the private investigator work then?"

"I already told you, it takes a license and all sorts of other stuff to be a PI. I'm just a background checker, court documents, things like that." I brushed a hint of errant sand off my shorts and kicked some more off my running shoes, thinking honestly that there were worse places to serve out this banishment, and worse jobs as well. I could hear Mark's voice as I considered my observation.

"Go down where it's warm, keep the income below a level they can touch, get a tan, sleep late every day, play around with this background-checking gig, and before you know it we'll have this whole thing reversed." He hadn't represented me at any time during the bankruptcy, but when the money was all gone (as were the lawyers) he'd signed on *pro bono* and hatched our little scheme. "The guys breathing on you are gonna realize they'll never get a dime this way and pretty soon they'll offer something. Or the judge will have his long-overdue heart attack. Before you know it you'll be back in business."

The Sun Provident Assurance Company didn't seem like a big insurance corporation, but it was. It had offices all along the Gulf Coast, and a sister enterprise hidden under a different name that ran almost up to Charlotte in the east and Chattanooga in the west. It peddled home, life, and auto insurance out of branch offices that were sometimes nothing more than trailers, kept the overhead low, and reaped a fortune off the volume. I received sporadic jobs from their office in the next town over from Exile, and on a slow day had done one of my standard corporate background checks to see who these folks actually were. That's how I found out that Sun Provident and its sister organization were actually part of the same entity.

There's a reason I'm good at this. My failed business, as Gray had so tactfully put it, was a computer software corporation that had put other businesses on the Internet. It was far more than mere Web site design, as we built packages for the clients' supply chain management, billing and payments, and anything else that they might need. Before you get the wrong idea and wonder whether ours was just another dot-com bomb, we had real customers, a real product, and real profits—until the promised Internet revolution fizzled. Maybe it's a bit much to say that it fizzled, but it certainly didn't take off like a rocket, and those of us with payrolls to meet, suppliers to pay, and loans that had to be serviced had expected just a bit more business than eventually resulted.

And if that sounds like an excuse, sue me. Everybody else has.

Anyway, quite a bit of the background information that I seek out is available on the Web, and so I feel at home doing the work I do now. The sad truth is that most of this is held in some obvious places, and if people like Harvey Webster of the Sun Provident Assurance Company would just bother to give it a try, they'd soon be doing what I do themselves and stop paying me for it.

Harvey Webster was at least fifty pounds overweight, with a walrus mustache and a thin ring of hair around the region of his ears. He didn't seem to understand that a bald man can do a lot for himself by getting into shape, or that a guy with a full head of hair and a beer belly is still considered a fatty. More specific to my involvement, he was so lazy that I doubt he would have gotten out of a chair to walk around if he smelled smoke, even in his own house.

I got to Harvey's trailer at nine-fifteen even though we'd agreed to meet at eight-thirty. I was still fifteen minutes early. Having worked with Harvey before, I was not surprised and simply sat in my car watching the bad part of town wake up.

"Come on in, come on in," Harvey said as I joined him at the door. Although the day's true heat was still five hours away, his short-sleeved business shirt was already soaked. He made me hold an oversized fast-food bag and a large coffee while he got the trailer's bright red door open. Inside, he dropped into an office-issue swivel chair and pushed a folder across at me before diving into the feed sack.

One of the good things about my current status is that I don't have to chase the work. I have spent a considerable amount of the last few months in the company of real private investigators, and they all work like dogs. Don't get me wrong; working like dogs has made some of these folks very wealthy, but this is the point where I have to remind you I am not trying to make money. So I sat there without making a move toward the folder until he finally put the cholesterol sandwich down and began to speak.

"This one's easy. Really just a check to make sure someone's not pulling a fast one on us. There was a hit-and-run in your neck of the woods—"

"In Exile?"

"Yeah." His voice trailed off, and I knew I had to reach for the file now. Harvey was not reliable when it came to the salient information on these jobs, and even though I wasn't looking to make big bucks I was not the least bit interested in running around in circles.

The folder contained the paperwork for a life insurance claim on a twenty-year-old man named Edward Gonzalez. The photocopied accident report said he'd been hit by a car while jogging—not in Exile, but Bending Palms, the next town over—and that the accident happened just after dark.

"You guys trying to get out of this one? Sounds pretty legit to me."

"Right, right, it's just a check, like I said. I mean, what's suspicious about a twenty-year-old unmarried guy buying life insurance and then collecting a full payout three weeks later?"

"So that's what got the attention of your home office."

"You gotta admit it's a little coincidental. And the last name doesn't help."

"Yeah, those rotten Hispanics are always arranging to get themselves run over so they can stick it to good old Sun Provident."

"You know what I mean."

"Harvey, I used to be in business with a gang of the most blue-blooded Wasps you'd ever want to lay eyes on, and one of the things it taught me is that cheating is not genetically encoded. Talent isn't, either, but that's another story."

I'd lost him a while back, so he picked up the sandwich again and asked if I was going to do the check or not.

As things turned out, I should have let it go. After all, I was doing this work primarily to keep my mind active and my hand in on the computer stuff while waiting for the situation up north to blow over. I couldn't use extra money, didn't like having anything to do with Harvey, and honestly didn't know very much about insurance. Something made me take this one, though, and I think it was the knowledge that Harvey and the good folks at Sun Provident were clearly angling to deny payment on what looked like the tragic end of a young life.

One of the odd by-products of my own legal misfortune was a heightened awareness of when it seemed to be happening to other people. I had decided at the outset that I wasn't going to be a part of anything like that. So my attitude was simple: No divorce work of any kind, obviously no bankruptcy-related investigations, and only the most basic insurance work. That might sound like the fledgling defense attorney who thinks he'll only handle innocent clients, but if you remember I wasn't trying to make any money, it sounds like it just might work.

It didn't, but it seemed that way at first.

Dennis Dannon was the Exile chief of police, and the first time we met I recognized him as one of the smartest people I would ever know. That had been when I first took up residence in his town, and being naive and unsure about my new "hobby" I decided to make a friend of the local law enforcement. So I went down to the small police station (five officers worked for Dannon, but only two were full-time) and introduced myself as someone who helped out private investigators from time to time.

Chief Dannon had been amused by this, but I had struck a chord with him and we had talked for close to an hour. It was only after I left that I realized he'd been more interested in my postbankruptcy state of mind, and it wasn't the first time I felt that Denny Dannon would have been a darn good psychiatrist. Tall and thin, he was a forty-something black man who had been born and raised in that little Gulf town. He'd left it only twice, and both of those excursions had been geared toward gaining him a spot on the Exile police force. He'd done a hitch in the navy as a shore patrolman in Diego Garcia and then earned an undergraduate degree in criminal justice at Florida State.

He was known to tell people that if he hadn't met his wife at State he would never have married, as he did not intend to leave Exile again. Instead of taking this as a slap at the quality of the local girls, the townspeople greeted this statement with pleasure and relief. They had seen too many of the town's brightest youngsters up stakes and never return, and it wore on them pretty hard.

I went to see Chief Dannon after leaving Harvey's office for the astounding reason that Harvey had not been completely wrong about Eddie Gonzalez's accident. It was true that Eddie's demise had not occurred in Exile, but the young man had been born and raised there, just like our chief of police. Dannon knew everyone and everything in his town, and I figured he'd be able to give me the straight skinny on the kind of kid Eddie Gonzalez had been.

Which turned out to be wrong. I walked in and explained what I was doing, conducting a little background check on the accident, and Dannon clammed right up.

"Not a chance, Frank. Eddie Gonzalez was a really good kid. His family is tops in my book, and your insurance friends are trying to get out of a contract. That's all this is, and I'm a little surprised at you for even coming in here."

He was seated behind his aluminum desk, dressed in the Exile police force uniform of gray shirt with matching pants and red piping. A tan park ranger–style brimmed hat hung on the ugly metal hat stand behind him, and under more pleasant circumstances I considered this a sharp uniform. Dannon didn't always wear it, oftentimes going around in civilian clothes with his star pinned to his shirt, but he didn't need even that for you to know he was the chief.

"That's really all I'm trying to establish, chief." I hadn't been offered a seat and remained standing. The walls of the tiny office were adorned with Dannon's diploma, various police certifications, and several pictures showing the people of Exile presenting him with awards. Another picture showed a head-and-torso shot of him as a teen in his white sailor's uniform, but it was scary how little he'd aged. "If I can show that this young man was a solid citizen, maybe they'll stop sniffing at this and just pay up."

He was condescending, a very different response than I was used to in that office, and I was beginning to wonder if I had misread the man.

"Frank, an insurance policy is a contract. On one side we have people paying their premiums, and on the other side we have the insurers paying out if something happens. The only problem with that is some insurers don't want to hold up their end of the agreement, and Sun Provident is by reputation one of the worst offenders. If I were you, I'd get copies of the official paperwork, go look at the SUV, wait a couple of days, and tell Harvey Webster that you didn't find a thing."

"SUV?"

"I'm not going to do your homework for you. Eddie was hit by a stolen SUV that was found dumped a few miles away by whoever did this. It was in the paper, so I suggest you go look it up."

Still puzzled at this development, I decided that I was getting dangerously close to alienating one of the big fish in the small pond of Exile and that I should leave. I nodded at Pete, one of the full-time cops on the force, as I walked through the outer office and headed for the door. I felt like a scolded schoolchild the entire way, and recognized the feeling because I'd experienced it a lot since my business died.

Once outside in the midday sun, I looked up and down the town's main street and began throwing ideas together. The heat reflected off of the sidewalk and began cooking me as I walked and thought. Maybe Dannon hated insurance companies, but then again, who didn't? Maybe he was just mad that Sun Provident was trying to renege on a legal contract, but then again, what else was new?

Another thought followed close on the heels of the first two. Maybe he was a bit suspicious himself about the timing of that insurance policy, but didn't want to let on because it might help Harvey get out of paying up. This did not fit the Denny Dannon that I knew, though, and I had rejected it before reaching the thin strip of park that ran through the middle of town. My car sat in the shade of one of the park's trees, and by the time I got to it I was rebuking myself for turning into a half-baked conspiracy theorist. My buddy Mark had warned me about that when he suggested I lie low down here.

"Just one thing. If you were anybody else, I'd suggest you go on welfare, hang out in the sun, and wait for the tide to turn. But a brain like yours needs things to do, and if you don't take it out for a walk every now and then, it will go walk itself. So a little background checking, a little court document retrieval, it'll make you feel good about yourself and keep your mind active. You may even come up with another one of those great patent ideas while you're waiting.

"So don't let this job assume a life of its own. It's a hobby, nothing else. Don't agree to go on stakeouts, don't let some Florida PI firm take you on as an apprentice, and don't start seeing things that aren't there. I work with some PIs from time to time, and you're not the type."

Having met a few PIs, I couldn't agree more, but I still had a job to do. And Denny Dannon's condescension hadn't helped, as it suggested that he considered me nothing but a mindless pawn in Harvey Webster's universe. There had to be a logical reason for this Eddie Gonzalez to have bought insurance not even a month before the accident, and if I could find it I could wrap this up to everyone's satisfaction. Including Chief Dannon.

I started with the part that I do best, the computer stuff. The Exile Public Library was a mile away on the other side of town, an old building that was loaded with very current hardware. Small as Exile might be, it was a well-run town, and it showed in places like the library.

The questions that needed answering were fairly obvious, and it sounded like they would quickly resolve this case in Eddie Gonzalez's favor. If he'd purchased insurance for a fraudulent reason it suggested he was afraid of imminent death, which could mean bad medical news or some kind of risky activity.

He had received a physical examination as part of Farragut Community College's application process, and he had passed with flying colors. Combined with his age, that seemed to rule out some kind of freak medical condition. The category of risky activity could be pretty broad, but in this case I could reasonably restrict it to some kind of dangerous criminal activity. That also seemed unlikely, going by what Chief Dannon had said, and I could definitely check it on the Web. Part of it, anyway.

Libraries have always been my sanctuary, and I had practically moved into the one in Exile when I first arrived. I was now living in a small one-story house near the beach, but in keeping with Mark's low-income scheme I didn't have a PC of my own, so I ghosted off of the computers in the library. I kept up with my e-mails in this way (using the town's only Internet cafe during off hours) and also met the reference librarian, Mary Beth Marquadt.

Mary Beth was almost one hundred and fifty years old and almost as smart as Chief Dannon. Once, when trying to impress a local PI with my discovery of the reference librarian's value, I had been almost laughed out of the place where we had been eating lunch. Apparently reference librarians are pretty much the same all over the country, and a sharp PI can get a lot of information in a distant city by dialing up the right custodian of the reference desk.

Mary Beth remembered Eddie Gonzalez fondly, and had attended his funeral the week before. According to her he was a bright kid, star track runner for Exile High, and quite sweet on a local girl named Anneliese Escobar. That fit nicely, as Anneliese was the beneficiary listed on the policy. Eddie had been attending Farragut Community College for the last two years, lived at home with his parents, and had been studying to become an accountant. Mary Beth's glowing recollection of him sounded almost the same as Chief Dannon's, and I was able to lay any suspicions about the chief's motives to rest just off that.

I then hopped on a terminal and accessed a site that would tell me if Eddie had any record of criminal behavior. A few jobs for a local law office had bought me a year's access to this particular site. Like anything else on the Web it runs the risk of being outdated or inaccurate, but it was a good place to start. As expected, I found nothing there.

Mary Beth had pulled back issues of local newspapers from the time of the accident by then, and I quickly read what was available. Exile did not have a town paper, so there was not much about Eddie's demise. He was hit by a stolen SUV just after dark while jogging on a popular oceanside fitness trail in the next town over. The Most-of-the-Coast fitness trail was used by bikers, joggers, and walkers. I went back to the Web and punched up a map of the trail, which ran through or touched on four towns and stretched along a thirty-mile segment of coast. I went back to the paper while the map was printing, and learned that the SUV had been found abandoned in a parking spot a few miles farther up the jogging trail.

Up the trail. That was odd. Eddie had been hit while crossing one of the many roads that intersected the bike path, presumably by joyriding car thieves, and I had to wonder why they hadn't peeled off to a better dumping spot. Amateurs, maybe. Locals, from the sound of it, if they knew of a parking spot a distance up the trail. I went and got the printed map, circling the page that contained an abbreviated line intersecting the path labeled "Finch Boulevard." That was where the accident occurred, and as the map indicated parking areas along the route, it wasn't hard to figure out where the SUV had been stashed.

I checked my findings with Mary Beth, who gave me some detail on the trail itself. She didn't know why I was so fixated on the path, but just from reading the papers I was getting an odd feeling that this didn't add up. It was easy to accept the confluence of events in which the joyriders crossed the route just as Eddie emerged from the foliage and stepped onto Finch Boulevard, but it didn't sound right that they would go on up the road and then double back to park the SUV along the trail. Obviously, they would want to get away from the vehicle as fast as possible, but weren't there better places to dump it?

Once again the Mark Ruben voice came into my head, warning me not to get crazy. According to the chief of police and a librarian who had watched him grow up, Eddie Gonzalez was a solid citizen with no enemies. He'd been hit by some fun-loving teens who had swiped a set of wheels and then dropped the SUV in what was probably a well-known necking spot on the bike path. It was no more sinister than the unfortunate timing of Eddie's insurance purchase.

Getting the computer information was my strong point and I was now left with the part I didn't do well at all. The databases would only get me so far. Sooner or later I was going to have to talk with a real live person. And not some clerk of the court, either. I was going to have to go talk with Eddie's family, and maybe even with the Escobars.

I looked forward to this the same way I look forward to hurting my foot, so I decided it might be better to go look at the site where it happened and where the vehicle had ended up. And if I went by the city impound lot to look at the vehicle, I might just eat up enough of the afternoon that I wouldn't have to go see any of those real live people for an entire day. Or even two.

CHAPTER TWO

The Most-of-the-Coast Fitness Trail had gone in where an old railroad track had been pulled out. Starting at a large state park ten miles east of Exile, it snaked along the shore to another park twenty miles west. Along the way it hugged the outside of several public beaches, detoured around some unfriendly places, like a shipyard and a liquid fuel facility, and even ran through the parking lots of some expensive shorefront condominiums.

The town to the west of Exile is called Bending Palms, an upscale place that you pass through on your way to the real money people in Davis. If you keep going you'll hit the beach-and-fun town of Panama City, then Pensacola as you're leaving the state, and before you know it you're in Mobile. The trail was really nice. It was as wide as a two-lane highway and paved with this rubbery blacktop that made it feel like artificial turf. A bright yellow line had been painted down the middle of it, and even though it needed to be redone, it was the only thing that was not in a tip-top state of repair. Much of the path was bordered by trees and wild scrub, also well maintained, and the crashing of the waves was never far away. Local businesses backed up right onto the path at some places, and some even catered to the fitness crowd.

At one bend in the trail a bike store had given itself two front entrances, one facing into the energetic town of Bending Palms and the other fronting on the path. It had painted advertising on the back walls of other buildings as you came down the trail, offering tire replacement and sodas along with hats and sunblock. Further into Bending Palms the fitness trail even boasted a juice bar with an outdoor area designed for the too-sweaty travelers of the trail.

Anything running thirty miles, even in a quiet part of the world like the Panhandle, is going to cut across a lot of streets. When the trail was right down on the ocean this wasn't much of a problem, but in the areas where it looped away it emerged from the trees onto what could sometimes be busy side streets and even a main boulevard or two. Finch Boulevard was one of the small side streets where the path looped away from the ocean.

I didn't get to the police impound lot that afternoon, instead spending the entire time on and around the trail. In fact, I stayed out there so long that when the sun began to set I went back to where the accident happened and parked in one of the circle 'P' spots on the map. It was perfectly located for observing the wooded area on either side of Finch Boulevard where a whole host of signs warned the drivers to be aware of people using the bike path.

If that weren't good enough, the segment of Finch Boulevard that was also the jogging trail was painted a dull yellow about the width of a car. I had inspected the area that afternoon, and going by the newspaper account it looked like a perfect place for an awful accident that would be nobody's fault. The road came around a gentle curve before passing the parking area, a flat cement strip whose boundaries were marked out by telephone poles laid on the ground.

I had back-and-forthed with my car several times, trying to get the best spot to observe the tragic crossing, before parking parallel to the road. When the car finally came to rest, I was facing the way the driver had faced when it happened. He would have come around the bend, come up on the crossing just a second or two later, and been unable to stop in time when Eddie came out of the woods on the left. Sitting off the road I could see up the trail for about twenty yards, but nobody driving on Finch Boulevard would have been able to see any part of the path either way.

That's why they posted the signs and painted the cement.

The dump spot still intrigued me. After watching the flow of bikers, joggers, and walkers crossing the street for an hour and noting that there weren't all that many of them once the sun started to go down, I drove the route I believed the SUV had taken. If the fleeing driver had continued up Finch Boulevard for a half mile, he would have run into an outside segment of the Bending Palms business district. That meant traffic lights, people, and maybe even a cop or two. So of course he took the first turn that avoided these hazards, and if he knew the area, he recognized he was headed parallel to the bike path, going the other way.

This was making a little more sense. Perhaps assuming a high level of panic on the driver's part explained the decision to double back and ditch the vehicle on the bike path. The driver had been desperate to separate from that SUV, and that supported the idea that it was a joyride gone wrong. After all, if the truck had been destined for the hold of a ship, the thief probably would have delivered it, Eddie or no Eddie. I was beginning to get happy about this, as it was all supporting the accident theory and I wanted Chief Dannon to see I wasn't helping the bad guys cheat Anneliese Escobar in her time of grief.

One of these days I'm going to have to sit down and figure out why the bankruptcy left me seeking the approval of complete strangers.

When I arrived at the dump site it looked a lot like the parking area where I had observed the intersection of Finch Boulevard and the jogging trail. It should have, being part of the fitness path itself, and the only difference was this segment was shielded from the side street by a solid row of trees. A low chain-link fence choked with brush ran alongside the road, and to actually observe whatever was going on in this particular turnout you had to drive into it.

And what teenager with a driver's license wouldn't know about a spot like that?

That night ended a lot like too many of the previous nights. My little rented house was nice enough, and the neighborhood was a quiet one, but somehow every time I came back there for the evening the place started to feel like a cell. Maybe it was because I was alone, and maybe it was because things were so quiet, but my thoughts invariably drifted back to the distant life that I used to lead up north.

Each night in Exile my routine would be to fix myself some kind of simple dinner if I didn't stop off and pick something up. Then I would settle down in front of the television and promise myself this time would be different, that I was going to watch the local news, or a sitcom, or a documentary, or anything other than the business news. And stirring something on the stove, or unpacking the Styrofoam carton containing my dinner, these thoughts would seem downright appealing.

They would stay that way as I got a soda from the old refrigerator and walked the entire ten feet from the center of my kitchen to the sofa in my living room. I even saw myself engrossed in the local events, or guffawing at some foolish comedy, eating my dinner and forgetting about what had happened. I remembered a time when I used to watch shows like that, and I found it easy to imagine myself watching them again.

Unfortunately, once the remote was in my hands the vision began to change. I did check the other channels, but it was a lot like ordering a big meal and then discovering I wasn't very hungry. I ran right through the news, and the comedies, and the documentaries, and before I knew it I was at one of the business shows. Sometimes I would flip on through, pretending I would not be back, but most times lately I would simply put the remote down and begin to watch in sick fascination.

Mostly I was hoping for some kind of headline about the state of bankruptcy law, some kind of miraculous reprieve that meant the long punishment was over, but even I knew that was not the way I would get that kind of news. It was hardly earth-shattering stuff to most of the world and so was not likely to be on the television. But I watched anyway, my heart rising and sinking every time the commentators gave a brief preview of what would be on next. And even when there was nothing related to my case in the offing, I would stay on that channel, soaking up the forecasts and debt ratings, the yield curves and the mergers.

Sometimes I woke up on that couch, early in the morning, with a replay of the same program running in front of me. Only when I was sure it was old news would I finally give in and go to bed.

Chief Bartholomew Tate of the Bending Palms Police Department would have been a Southern caricature if it were not all an act. The Bending Palms police force wore khaki uniform shirts, and Tate's belly presented itself from behind his with great authority. He was pushing sixty years of age, but he was a big man and looked like he concealed a fully functional pile of muscles behind the fat.

He reached across the beechwood counter in the station as I approached, smiling as he took my hand and telling me why he knew who I was.

"You must be Mr. Frank Cole, from our sister township of Exile.

Denny Dannon called me about you just yesterday, said you'd probably be by." His voice was a jovial, booming lilt that told the world he could act this way because he was the chief. "Come on back to my office."

The sun was shining in through a massive set of windows fronting on Main Street, and I wondered if having the station in the center of town was a Southern thing or just a small-town thing as I followed the chief.

"Set down there, I've got what you need right here." He dropped into a large wooden swivel chair behind a matching, expensive-looking desk. His office was paneled in wood, numerous fish were mounted on small plaques on the walls, and the rest of the space looked like a copy of Denny Dannon's office.

"Denny told me to call you some dirty names before giving this to you, but that's just a couple of good ol' boys havin' fun with one of our newer Yankees." Tate held a manila file folder in his hands, but made no move to give it to me. "He also said you seem like an all-right guy but the jury's still out on you, so I hope you'll keep it quiet when I tell you ol' Denny took this accident a little personal."

He nodded with big hunting-dog eyes, and I had the sense not to interrupt.

"I'd never met this boy, but Denny knew him well, and he sure did want to know who did this. Asked me to have the boys dust the inside of that SUV. We don't normally do that in these cases, and as you might expect it was wiped clean. We asked around with all the teen hard cases, even went to the schools nosin' around for rumors, but there was nothing."

He leaned forward, offering the folder.

"I think everything you need is right in there. Accident report, fingerprint results, theft report on the SUV, the works." Again with the hunting-dog eyes. "If you'd like to go see it, I'll run you over there."

In comparison with my frosty reception at the Exile police station, this was more than a little different. Had Dannon felt bad about the way he handled me the day before, or was this just one of those things that police forces in neighboring towns did for each other? I was still new to this.

"Where is your impound lot, sheriff?" It seemed natural to call him that even if it was a mistake.

"Oh, we don't have an impound, son. We kept that four runner out back here for a few days until it was obvious even to Denny that we weren't gonna catch anybody, and then we returned it to the lot it came from. Jason's Subaru, on the other side of town."

"Subaru? I didn't know it was stolen from a lot."

"Well, it was sitting in Jason's overflow area, was a trade-in that he hadn't unloaded yet, and you know how these things work. Leave something sitting still long enough, someone's gonna steal it. Heck, if it hadn't been for the accident ol' Jason probably wouldn't have noticed it was gone for another month."

He reached for the same kind of hat the Exile cops wore, signaling it was time to go. I had chased down numerous police reports and field cards in my time as a fact-checker, and there was a nominal fee involved in most places.

"How much for all this, chief?" I asked, holding the folder up. I still hadn't opened it.

He slapped a big hand on my shoulder, turning me toward the door as we exited into the main office.

"Forget about it this time around, boy. We just use that for coffee money anyway."

The SUV stood on the exact spot from which it had been stolen. It was jet-black, one of those gas-guzzling monsters that you see bombing around the highways like the drivers are assaulting Fortress Europe,

It had one of those absurd cowcatcher, DEA-knock-the-front-door-down grille protectors, also black, and apart from a few scratches on it you couldn't tell it had been in an accident.

What stood out immediately was the smoked-glass windows. Just short of being too dark to be legal, they went all the way around and included the windshield. No wonder the driver didn't see Eddie Gonzalez until he was under the tires.

Chief Tate stood off to the side while Lester Jason of Jason's Subaru unlocked the front door. As far as a background check was concerned this was going above and beyond, but I was trying to gather up every shred of evidence that this had been an accident, and the darkened windows were definitely a plus in that category. I slipped behind the wheel just for a moment, as it was hotter than heck in there, and even though I was looking into the sun I didn't have to squint.

"I thought having that much tint in a window was illegal," I said to the chief while Lester locked up the truck again. We were standing in the overflow lot of the Subaru dealership, a dirt patch in back of the building and far out of sight of the people looking at the shiny new cars.

"Windshield and driver's side, probably yes, even though this shade's close. Who owned this, Lester? One of those bad old drug dealers?"

Lester was a thin man who seemed very nervous around the law, or maybe around insurance people asking questions. He shrugged.

"Been here for almost a month, recent trade-in. One of the mechanics said he might want to buy it. I can check to see who owned it."

"Just joshing you, Les. Somebody noticed it was sitting here is all, and it wasn't the old owner." He adjusted his belt while looking around the small yard. "Chain-link fence without a gate, visible from the street but not from inside. Les, if I was a suspicious man I'd wonder if you were hoping this heap would walk off on you."

He winked playfully at me, but I knew he was basically dictating this segment of my report and I began to wonder just how dumb Chief Dannon had said I was. Lester seemed to have lost interest in the conversation, and the chief bade him good day while we walked back to his car. As we were driving the six blocks back to the station I decided to practice asking leading questions.

"Looks pretty straightforward to me, chief. Anything strike you as unusual about any of this?"

"Yep." He turned into the station parking lot where my old Honda sat cooking in the sun. "Nothing big, but it did seem to be an odd place to go joyriding. Finch Boulevard's residential at one end and business district at the other. Most of the hoot-and-holler stuff we see happens close to the highway or down by the tracks."

He smiled at me over the top of the car as we got out.

"But then again, who knows with kids like that? Maybe they were picking up a friend, maybe they stopped off in a quiet side street to smoke a little evil weed. Who knows?" He looked down at the pavement and then back up at me, this time without the smile. "Just bad luck is all. You say hi to Chief Dannon for me when you see him next, Frank."

The whole thing seemed to wrap up about then, which is why I decided to take it apart again. Maybe it was the obvious handling I was receiving from the local law, maybe it was the nagging question about the timing of that insurance policy, and maybe it was Chief Tate's remark about the location of the accident, but the biggest thing I can point to is it *seemed* wrong.

So back to the drawing board, or in my case the chessboard, as I figured my new buddy, Gray Toliver, might own the set of unbiased eyes I needed. He was beating the stuffing out of another retiree when I walked up to our spot on the Exile town promenade. I waited for the match to end and listened to the waves. The sand down here is almost white, and it packs quite a glare if you stare at it for long in the mid-afternoon sun. Gray finished up with his latest opponent in no time and I wandered over.

"Can't fit you in for a game right now, Frank. Sorry." He started to pack the heavy pewter chess pieces away in a small wooden case. The heavier pieces did much better in the wind than the cheap plastic ones I would have brought, and they were cool-looking to boot.

"I didn't come for a game, Gray," I said, swinging a leg over the concrete bench and sitting down.

It didn't take more than a few minutes to bring Gray up to speed, and he stopped me when I got to the suggestion that Chief Dannon seemed a bit too worked up about a simple vehicular homicide.

"Nah, Denny Dannon's all right. He's just a little offended that something like this happened to two of the nicer families in Exile. It's a funny thing about small-town cops, Southern cops in particular. If they stay on the job long enough, or become chief, they pretty much adopt the town and everybody in it. And as for Tate, he and Dannon have been backing each other up for years, a little extra manpower when it's needed. Just last year Dannon was chasing a hot-rodder all over the back roads one night when fights started at two different bars at opposite ends of town. Tate and a couple of his people were over there as soon as the phone rang, and Dannon's done the same for Tate at different times.

"So no, there's nothing out of the ordinary there. And maybe your little accident case is just that, an accident like everybody thinks it is." He gave me a meaningful look. "But I don't think so."

I leaned forward. Except for Harvey, Gray was the only person who thought something might be out of line here.

"What makes you say that?"

"You do. Frank, I spent the last twenty years designing airplane wings, still do a little contract work out at Pensacola when there's a question about a wing I worked on, and during those years I learned to trust my little voices. It's like when you write up a list of things you need at the store, get your wallet, and walk out to the car thinking something's not quite right. And when you get to the store you find out you left that silly checklist on the kitchen table. That's what was wrong, and a voice was telling you so.

"You think something's wrong because it actually is. You just can't put your finger on it yet, but if you keep going, it'll pop up."

Reassuring as the words were, they didn't tell me what to do next.

"Gray, what would you do right now? How would you find out what's wrong?"

"That's easy. Stop asking what *is* wrong, and ask what *could* be wrong. Keep the net wide on that, because it's going to help you cross a whole bunch of possibilities off the list while you're looking at them." From my expression he could tell I needed a little more than that. "How about this? Eddie Gonzalez had himself killed for the insurance money. Don't repeat that to anybody, by the way; I still have to live in this town and even though I don't know them, the Gonzalez family is well thought of. So why would a young man want himself dead?"

"He didn't have anything medically wrong with him; Sun Provident got a copy of the physical he took when he entered Farragut Community College. From what everybody says, he had a bright future and a steady girlfriend, so he probably didn't want to kill himself. He was never in trouble with the law, so unless he was living a double life I don't think he arranged for this."

"There you go. Cross one off the list. And as a little backup to your conclusion, it's doubtful a man living with his parents, going to school all day, and seeing his girl every night was living a double life. But you're on the right track now. Look at every possibility and scratch them off one at a time." He looked at his watch and stood up abruptly. I had kept him from wherever he was headed when I first came up.

"Thanks a lot, Gray."

"Anytime. You just needed a different set of ears to hear the same story." He stuck his hand out, something he hadn't done since we first met, and shook mine firmly. "Good luck with this, Frank, but remember, sometimes the wrong thing you're looking for is no more important than a shopping list left on the kitchen table. What I'm trying to say is, this might still end up as just an accident, and after all, it's just a little insurance job. Don't go getting yourself all worked up about it."

He was walking toward his car when he turned and called gently, "But let me know how it turns out. I love puzzles."

Rosario Gonzalez was Eddie Gonzalez's father, and neither his given name nor his surname seemed to fit him. A white oval patch on the chest of his work shirt said "Rosie" in red letters, matching the trim around the patch, and when he spoke it was without an accent of any kind. Tall and thick, he looked like a dark-haired guy with a good tan and was friendly right from the start.

I had figured the dead boy's parents might be slightly more amenable to talking with an insurance company representative than would, say, the boy's beneficiaries, and I was right for once. At the same time, though, the Gonzalez family had suffered the loss of their only son and I wouldn't have been a bit surprised if they hadn't wanted to speak to me this side of perdition.

So I was both pleased and surprised to discover that Rosie had left me a phone message at home, returning the call I had placed to his house before going to see Gray. He had asked me to come down to his garage that afternoon if possible. I found it easily enough, having driven by it numerous times and never registering the Gonzalez Gas and Repair sign that ran in huge red letters over the three-bay maintenance area and the office. The place was clean, the equipment looked new, and three mechanics were working on three different cars when I walked up.

"Thanks for coming down, Mr. Cole. Anything we can do to help out the Escobars, you just name it." He shook my hand with a grip that could have turned a rusted lug nut, and I just stood there looking stupid for several seconds before telling him to call me Frank. Just after that I was sitting in his office with a soda, listening to one of his helpers work a hydraulic jack, and wondering if I had the right Rosie Gonzalez.

"Mr. Gonzalez, let me start by offering my deepest sympathies. I know this must be very hard on you."

His face showed almost no reaction, but he leaned forward in his seat and pointed an unoffending finger in my direction as he spoke.

"Call me Rosie. I knew you were a good man the moment I heard your voice on the machine, and here you go and prove it by offering your sympathies. You know, I was wondering when somebody from the insurance company was going to want to talk to me, and honestly I was getting a little annoyed that so far you folks only talked to the Escobars. But you've made it all right now, and don't worry about my boy Eddie. He's in a good place." He lowered the finger and smiled fraternally.

I have got to get better at responding to completely unexpected developments.

No one from Sun Provident had been in contact with the dead boy's family. You could have knocked me over with a feather.

"Well, I apologize for not getting by sooner, sir, but I just got the file the other day and I've been talking to Chief Dannon—"

"A good man."

"Absolutely. And he speaks very highly of your entire family." He nodded pleasantly and I got the impression he felt he wasn't letting me talk. "I just wanted to ask you a couple of questions, background mostly, to wrap up the case. For instance, did your son go jogging on that path a lot?"

"Yes, he was very serious about staying in shape. He won all sorts of medals running for Exile High School." A catch in his throat said Rosie wasn't quite as adjusted to the accident as he let on, but it actually reassured me a little. It had only been a couple of weeks, after all.

"Every day?"

"Well, during the semester he ran in the mornings before going to school, just about every day."

"Mornings?" I was writing feverishly on a notepad.

"Yes, but he had to stop that when school ended for the summer and he had to be up early for his job."

"So he didn't normally run in the evening?"

"No." The older man got a faraway look in his eye at that. "That must have been the second or third time he went running at night. You see, every summer he painted houses with his cousin Davie, he'd been doing that for years. They had just started this season's work when it happened."

His voice was losing the timbre it had contained when I started the conversation, but I was pretty sure I had stumbled across the oddity that Gray had told me to think about and wanted to pursue it.

"Sir, did your son go running every night at the same time?"

"Yes, at least those few times. His cousin likes to hit the bars right as the sun goes down, so he was home pretty much the same time every night."

"Did he think this was dangerous? Did he ever mention having a close call, like almost getting hit by a car?"

"Oh no, Frank, that was pretty impossible."

"Why is that, sir?"

"Anneliese gave him a big orange reflector vest"—he smiled at this, a happy memory—"with reflective stripes. You could see that silly thing from across town."

"This is his girlfriend, Anneliese?"

"Well, fiancée really. After all, you can't bring a child into the world without getting married, can you?"

He said it in such an offhand fashion that I almost missed it. I am really going to have to practice my response to completely unexpected answers, because my astonishment must have been all over my face when I comprehended what he'd said. Rosie smiled at me with that easy expression on his face.

"I'm sorry, Mr. Cole, I didn't know you didn't know. Anneliese is three months' pregnant with my grandchild. They were going to get married next month, but, thank goodness, they decided to get the insurance a little early. I mean"—he indicated the business around us with his hands—"I'm doing all right, and Escobar's actually a little ahead of me, but taking care of a baby costs a lot of money."

He stopped talking, turning his head and fixing me with a look that was somewhere between puzzlement and suspicion.

"Didn't you know that, Mr. Cole?"

Those of us in the information business sometimes forget about the Harvey Websters of the world. While we're out there trying very hard to provide our clients with timely and accurate facts, guys like Harvey are frequently asleep at the switch. This seemed to be one of those times, and even though Rosie offered to take me over to meet the Escobars I really didn't think that was necessary anymore.

A twenty-year-old unmarried college man does not buy life insurance unless he has an undisclosed terminal illness or is running with some very dangerous people, or trying to defraud the good people of Sun Provident Assurance. That is, unless his fiancée is pregnant and he's getting ready to embark on the life of a married man with a child, a house, a car, and a metric ton of financial obligations.

Harvey actually was asleep when I burst into the trailer. It was a hot Florida afternoon, and I was pretty well lathered by the time I got there. Add in my personal dislike for Harvey and my certainty that the case was closed in the Escobars' favor, and it made for fine theatre. I stormed straight up and slapped at his feet just as he was pulling them off the desk, hitting a small pile of papers stacked on the in box. They sailed up into the path of his oscillating fan and headed for the ceiling.

"Hey, there, Harv! Guess what I found out?"

He blinked at me in answer, but since I wasn't really waiting for his reply, I kept going.

"Anneliese Escobar is pregnant, *hermano!* Expecting, with child, eating for two, and I'll give you three guesses who the father was."

"Gonzalez? The dead guy?"

"Lightning-fast deduction, as always, Harv. Yes, Eddie Gonzalez was the father. They were going to get married, and like a responsible groom he bought his bride and inbound child a little security. Pretty smart of him, considering how things turned out."

He looked as if he were turning this over in his mind, so I took the opportunity to flop down in an armless chair and got to the point.

"Harvey, why didn't you guys know this? Didn't you even talk with her?"

It was my turn to be surprised, watching his face wrinkle up as if something smelled bad.

"Talk with her? Talk with her? Why? They just filed the claim a few days ago, Cole. We're in the fact-checking stage of things, in case you forgot that was what we asked you to do." He was regaining his footing, letting the Sun Provident Assurance Company Field Manual do his thinking for him. He grabbed a pen. "Now, who told you this?"

"Rosie Gonzalez, Eddie's father. You can call and check that, but don't let me hear that you were rude to him. He might not sound like it, but he took the loss pretty hard." I slapped my thighs. "Now, in my book this one's finished. You guys wanted to know why Eddie bought the insurance, and now you've got an answer. I'm going to go get a nice meal, maybe swim in the ocean before the sun goes down, and tomorrow you'll have my report.

"So I want my fee when I walk in, not like last time." I'd waited patiently for three weeks before asking on the last job, and then wore out Harvey's carpet for two more months before they finally cut me a check. It had been a measly seventy-five dollars, too, so I hit them with the full rate this time. "One-fifty, for pounding the pavement for two days and scaring up the police work as well."

"Sure, sure, Frank, whatever you say." Harvey seemed preoccupied at this point, and even though it should have made me suspicious I just assumed he was thinking about supper. I never should have mentioned food if I wanted to keep his attention. He stood up and extended his hand, and I shook it.

I was feeling pretty darn good about myself as I wheeled the Honda back toward my house. The sun was still two hours in the sky, and living two blocks away from a public beach made a late afternoon swim sound like a nice idea. There was a little roadside restaurant that I sometimes went to up the highway, a quiet place with an outstanding Cajun seafood pasta dish, and I decided to treat myself to that tonight in celebration.

The truth was that I had been feeling lousy for weeks and had even started wondering about packing up and going back up north. My first few months in Florida had been pretty rough, as the loss of my business had done awful things to my confidence, and Mark's plot against my creditors felt more like running away than legal maneuvering. That had passed when I got my first few gigs and had to focus on things like finding the right courthouse and making friends with the clerks. I had even developed a modest pride in quickly locating the necessary information, but that had not lasted.

In the meantime I got the distinct feeling that the world was passing me by while I played chess with Gray, sat on the beach, and tried to get cozy with the local law. There had been less and less movement on my appeal, and Mark had made ominous comments regarding his surprise that my creditors had not made so much as a peep in what was quickly approaching a year.

So the Gonzalez case perked me up. It had started badly with the misguided attempt to enlist Chief Dannon's aid, but good, dogged investigating had yielded up a satisfactory conclusion, just as Gray had said it would. I reminded myself to call him as I walked through the front door of the cracker box that I called home.

And saw the bullet sitting straight up and insolent on my kitchen table.

I know nothing about guns and never intend to so much as handle one, so you can bet the bullet was not mine and had not been there that morning. I looked around the place quickly, which wasn't hard, because it was nothing more than a kitchen, living room, bath, and bedroom on the same floor.

There was no sign of entry other than the knuckle-sized missile on the kitchen table, a copper-colored bullet sitting in a golden cartridge case. The top of the round mated perfectly with the shell beneath it. I slowly went closer and saw for the first time that the bullet stood on a small piece of paper. Someone had carefully cut the article from some Florida paper about the hit-and-run death of a twenty-year-old Exile man named Edward Gonzalez.

The good feeling of just a few minutes before evaporated, and I began to feel as if people were watching me through the windows.

"But I'm just a fact-checker," I whispered in a voice that was not my own.

CHAPTER THREE

If the message-in-a-bullet people had held off on their visit for just two days I never would have figured this mess out. A surprising number of things happened in those forty-eight hours, and by the dawn of the third day I had so many people mad at me that it could have been any of them.

But at that moment there was absolutely no call for anyone to threaten me over this little fact-checking assignment, and, near as I could tell, I had resolved it to the satisfaction of everyone who mattered. In the meantime the edges of that newspaper clipping had been scissored out with laserlike precision, the bullet looked as if it had never been touched by human hands, and the absurdity of the whole scene suggested that I had somehow crossed into an entirely different and very alien territory.

Sun Provident hadn't left me that bullet, Rosie Gonzalez certainly hadn't, and I had not even met the Escobars. So whoever had done this was some total unknown, someone in the shadows, someone who took great pains to do things perfectly. They hadn't broken a window to get into my place, they had touched nothing, and when I briefly considered calling Chief Dannon I saw that it was very likely he wouldn't believe me. Whoever had done this was thinking everything through with great clarity, and even though they wanted to make sure I got the message, they didn't want any more police involvement than had already occurred.

Gray had told me to consider every possible way that an SUV had been made to occupy the same space as Eddie Gonzalez, and one of the possibilities that had occurred to me was that it was a pure, stupid mistake. Not an accident, mind you, but a murder that had nailed the wrong man. And now I had to go back to that theory, because whoever put that bullet on my kitchen table was very serious about scaring me off the trail. Serious because it had not been an accident.

The tinted glass was what suggested this most strongly. The SUV had sported a complete set of smoked-glass windows and windshield, tinted so dark that it would have been pretty easy to hit a jogger who only resembled the intended victim. Stealing a vehicle with that level of tinting had turned out to be a mistake for the murderer, even though he had picked the vehicle for that very reason. No matter how soon he dumped it, he was going to be driving the vehicle a certain distance after the accident and sure didn't want to be identified by a chance witness. So the tinting had been for his protection and had been as desirable in the stolen vehicle as the heavy cowcatcher on its front.

I had dismissed this idea for the stupid reason that it was simply too big a coincidence for someone to hit the only guy on the jogging trail who had just purchased insurance. And it would have stayed dismissed if it weren't for that bullet.

You see, the tale of a teenager joyriding in a stolen vehicle, hitting a jogger by accident, and stashing the SUV in a nearby lovers' turnout made perfect sense unless you looked at it from this angle: If you were a reasonably prudent individual trying to commit a murder, this was one of the ways you might do it. You wouldn't use a weapon like a gun because it would leave ballistic and gunpowder evidence. You wouldn't use a knife because you could get marked with the blood. You'd use a big, heavy truck with a protective grille and darkened windows.

You wouldn't steal this vehicle from in front of someone's home like a joyrider would, simply because you'd be worried it wouldn't be there on the night you needed it. No, you'd pick a truck that was always sitting in the same spot. And after the accident you'd ditch it as soon as possible, probably parking right next to the car that would take you away from the whole thing.

Most importantly, you'd recognize that there is no such thing as a perfect crime and that if enough people look at something long enough, they will figure it out. And so you'd do the next best thing and make it look like an accident. The perfect murder is the one no one investigates.

The bullet said that someone had become worried about my investigating this one.

I began functioning on a very basic level for the next couple of days after that. The most primal reaction we have is to flee, and in a way that's exactly what I did. That might sound like an overreaction on my part, but I had no way of knowing what was likely to happen next. Maybe someone was just trying to scare me. Then again, who knew what other accidents they might be able to arrange?

So off I went. If anyone was watching, they saw me pack a small bag, get into the car, and drive off in the direction of the highway. If they wanted me to get out of town, at the very least I was going to make them think they'd succeeded. I made sure I hadn't been followed before doubling back and finding a nice secluded spot near the beach to spend the night. After all, I'd already shaved my existence down to such an extent that I owned almost nothing, and so the final step to living in my car wasn't half as big a stretch as it is for anyone living a normal life.

Oddly enough, the first night, I slept in one of the parking areas along the fitness trail. It was not a comfortable night, as the bugs got in if I cracked the window even a notch and it was unbearably hot if I didn't, but I already knew what I was going to do in the morning, and it involved the fitness trail.

When I blew into Exile nine months earlier, I lived in a low-rent trailer park at the edge of town, sleeping in my car, and so I was familiar with the spots where a man can shower and shave for free. I needed to look presentable for the day's work, and after downing some coffee and a greasy breakfast sandwich at a roadside stand I set off on my task.

I think I already mentioned that the fitness trail sometimes went right through the parking lots of some pretty expensive rental properties, and so that was where I was headed. If I had been a real PI and had believed Eddie Gonzalez to be the victim of foul play, these probably would have been the first places I visited. However, I am not a PI, didn't think the hit-and-run was anything but an accident, and was only doing background for a slipshod insurance outfit. That is, before the bullet arrived on my kitchen table.

The apartments were important for two reasons: First, they undoubtedly had some security or maintenance personnel, and second, they would probably have surveillance cameras in their parking lots. I was only concerned with the properties a few miles on either side of the accident site because I wanted to see if some of the surveillance footage showed runners going through the edge of the lot. I was hoping for something out of the ordinary, but if I got lucky there just might be a tall man with dark hair and a shiny reflector vest who ran that path right around twilight most nights.

Having encountered nothing but hostility when I told people I was running down an insurance claim, I decided to modify my story without turning it into a complete lie. Just after nine I walked up to the management office of the first set of apartments, a garish pink stucco colony festooned with video cameras. An old man wearing suspenders over a dirty work shirt greeted me by saying the manager was not yet in.

"Well, maybe that's for the better, sir." I extended my hand and smiled the way I used to smile at prospective investors. "I bet you're in charge of part of this complex, and I'm guessing security. Am I right?"

He straightened up right away, shifting from one foot to another briefly before explaining with pride that he was actually in charge of maintaining the grounds.

"I knew it. Like my father used to say, you want to know how an outfit runs, find the guys who actually do the work and talk to them. I bet there isn't a thing that goes on around here that you don't know about."

"Well, I can't say I see everything, Mr.—"

"Cole, sir, Frank Cole. I do a little investigating work in this part of the world."

"Well, I'm Todd Stanley, Mr. Cole, and like I said I do the maintenance around here. Did you say you were a private investigator?"

I leaned forward as if conspiring with him in that empty office.

"Actually, this one here is related to an accident about ten days ago. It happened a little way up the jogging path that borders the property—"

"Oh, that hanged trail! I can't believe we have to put up with that! Legalized trespass, what that is. And you should see what kind of people just come strolling right into our parking lot off of that thing, Mr. Cole, vagrants, drug people, joggers relieving themselves against my Dumpsters. It's a crying shame . . ."

I let him go on. It just made sense that the fitness trail would be a source of concern and annoyance to the staff and residents of such a place, and I was ready to play on it. I let him finish telling me about all the evil people who used that jogging path and then launched into my story.

"You know, Mr. Stanley, that accident was just waiting to happen. I'm investigating this whole situation for an insurance company whose name has to stay confidential, I'm sure you already knew that, but I can tell you that the insurance bonds of several municipalities are in danger because of this fitness trail."

"Really?"

"Absolutely. The liability hazard is enormous. None of the crossing areas is properly marked, no stoplights, it was just a matter of time until someone got hurt."

"Oughta have gates and flashing lights, just like a railroad crossing."

"Wouldn't we like to see that." I nodded importantly at him while trying not to get sidetracked by the laughable mental picture he'd given me. "Now, as you already know, making those crossings safe would cost the neighboring towns and cities quite a bit of money—"

"Oh, they don't like to hear things like that!"

"No, they don't, sir. So my company asked me to come take a look and see if there might not be some other reason, in addition to the danger of the street crossings, to"—I whispered at this point—"discontinue the jogging path entirely."

I was his savior. He cocked his head to the side, and his mouth hung slightly open in rapture at the very thought. If the rest of the staff at the other complexes were even half as eaten-up as this guy was, I'd have no trouble accessing their surveillance footage. Now to find out how far back they kept the tapes.

"Now, Todd— May I call you Todd? Excellent. You go ahead and call me Frank. I noticed video cameras directed toward the section of your parking area that borders the fitness trail . . ."

I won't bore you with the work I put in over the next two days. As things turned out it was just as well that I was leading my fugitive existence on the fitness trail, because there was plenty of videotape to observe and time was scarce. I needed to be close to where I was working. At first I restricted my tape viewing to the last hour before the sun went down, but Todd's complex had footage going back three weeks and I had to chop it down to a half hour just to keep my focus.

We've all seen key moments of surveillance footage on cop shows and news broadcasts, the seconds when the car thief approaches the bait or the shoplifter actually pockets the merchandise, but most of us don't understand just how tough it is to sit through the hours of tape where nothing happens. In my case it was worse, as I was watching replay where I knew nothing had happened and I wasn't even sure of what I was seeking. Obviously I wanted to identify people who seemed to use the trail every night so I could talk to them about anything they might have seen out of the ordinary, but in addition to that I wanted to get a good look at the folks who only appeared once or twice prior to the accident.

The guys who had sent me the Smith & Wesson telegram were meticulous people, and if they had plotted the accident with the same kind of precision, they would have spent some time on the trail itself. Todd's community was the only one with recordings going back very far, but one of the others had two weeks' worth, and so I spent a considerable time stopping, starting, rewinding, and making notes about the action as it passed before me. Even when nothing was happening I was learning what normal people did on the trail, hoping that my new friends would stick out like a sore thumb if they showed up on the footage doing their reconnaissance work weeks before.

My white lie about inspecting the fitness trail for possible closure had gotten me access to the tapes of three communities on the route, two in Bending Palms on either side of the incident and one farther up the coast in Davis. I had been brusquely refused at another complex, but there really is a limit to how much pedestrian traffic film a lone man can watch and so I had hunkered down to really go over what I had. Todd made his own viewing equipment available to me in his shed, one of the other two compounds actually let me borrow their tapes, and the third let me run their originals over to a photo shop and make copies. So I not only had a spot to do my mundane work, but I was also out of sight.

This turned out to be important, as explained by my answering machine when I called up from a pay phone down near the beach. I didn't really expect too many messages, as I had no other work and didn't receive a lot of calls when I did. I had not bothered going to see Harvey to collect my fee, fearing that he might have blabbed my name to the wrong people and having no written report to give him anyway, and so he was not one of the people who called in my absence.

Rosie Gonzalez did, though, and his message told me not to expect to hear from Harvey anytime soon.

"Mr. Cole, I don't know what to think here. I thought you were a good guy, but the Escobars just got word from your insurance company that their claim was on hold because of something you said about Eddie. I don't want to discuss this with a machine, but I can't imagine what you might think you found and I want to meet with you right away."

He left me with his work, home, and cell numbers as well as a feeling that I had been badly used by one Harvey Webster. The only bright moment in the whole investigation had been my explanation of Eddie Gonzalez's insurance purchase, and I had even hoped that news of the policy's resolution might get the bullet fairy off my trail.

But now all that was down the drain. I was still scratching down the last numbers Rosie had given me when the next message came on. It was Dannon, and he sounded displeased.

"Mr. Cole, I need to see you right away. It seems you reported something to the Sun Provident people about Eddie being involved in gambling up at the college, and I have to tell you that if you can't substantiate that, I will personally make sure you never work as an investigator again. I thought I told you that Eddie was a good guy, but maybe I wasn't clear on that. At any rate, call me at any time at the following number."

I didn't get a single digit of that one, as his statement set my head spinning in a way that even the monotonous fitness trail movies had not. Gambling at Farragut College? Who mentioned gambling? I hadn't gone near the college, which was surprising because I was enrolled in a weekly photography class there which I had just missed for the first time. My fugitive status had made my attendance seem unwise, and here I was supposed to have unearthed some false information in a place I was afraid to visit. In the meantime, Dannon's suggestion that he'd explained anything to me when I'd visited him three days earlier chapped me considerably. I recalled the meeting as a firm brush-off and wondered how he was suddenly seeing it as a full and revealing interview that even a moron like me could understand.

The last message was the best. It was from Anneliese Escobar's brother Mike, and if the guys who broke into my place had waited a couple of days I would have assumed the bullet message had been from him.

"Hi there. This is Michael Escobar, Anneliese Escobar's brother, and if you'd bothered to come by and talk to us you'd know I work in one of the biggest law firms in northern Florida"—I already knew that, even though he forgot to say he was just a paralegal—"and that we don't take any abuse from guys like you. I pulled your bankruptcy case off the legal databases, and you've got some nerve pointing fingers at a dead man after what you did to your employees up north.

"So you listen to me, buster. You better get with those Sun Provident crooks and straighten this thing out. Or you better run back up north. If I ever catch you on the street—"

The tape ran out a little after that, but let's skip the grisly details. He should have known better than to make threats of bodily harm into a recording device, but right then the shortcomings of his legal training were not my highest concern. I hung up with my heart pounding and leaned heavily against the cinder block wall of the beach snack stand whose phone it was.

There was a lot of bad information to process in those messages, but the first question that popped up was easily the most important: Who had given out so much detailed information on a flagged insurance claim? Normally you have to hold insurance people down and pull out their teeth just to get them to refer you to their managers, and yet everyone seemed to know just what was causing all the ruckus and even who was supposed to have provided that information. In an industry where stonewalling is the rule and the hope is that a beneficiary will get frustrated and go away, who would be shelling out all the facts?

Harvey.

I stopped off at a construction site on my way to Harvey's trailer. I knew I was taking a big chance in going to the very place where I had received the job in question, a spot probably being watched by the guys who let the bullets do their talking, but I knew Harvey wouldn't give me the truth over the phone. At the work site I quickly located what I needed, a brand-new common nail that I picked up with a handkerchief. Just before heading up the steps to Harvey's door I propped the nail up against the passenger side front tire of his car with the point up. I figured Harvey might be watching me from a window when I left, and was reasonably sure that he would still deserve a punctured tire even after we were done talking.

Good thing, too, as he wasn't alone. I opened the door gently enough, hoping to get answers and figuring it would do no good to go in shouting, but I stopped almost immediately. A red-faced man in his forties, wearing the same kind of light coat-and-tie outfit I was wearing, looked at me in obvious recognition. He smiled like the schoolyard bully and said, "Well, there he is."

That phrase has bad connotations for me ever since the business died. I was walking into a law firm, one of the many outfits representing the people I owed money to, and some wiseguy law school grad, so young that he wouldn't handle a case for years, looked up and said, "Well, there he is."

Only he didn't say it in a normal way, the easy fashion in which you would point out a relative at a crowded airport arrival gate. He didn't even say it as if he were going to take part in the scheduled deposition and I was a minute or two late. No, he said it the same way you'd say, "Well, there he is, the guy who stole the wheelchairs from the old folks' home."

As this past episode was a voluntary deposition and I was finally waking up to the fact that I was getting shafted, I turned to my lawyer and told him that he should never have agreed to do this on the other guy's territory and stomped out, deposition untaken. In business I go by the idea that if I want to talk to you I come to see you, and if you want to talk to me you come and see me, but in any case you keep a civil tongue in your head.

I disliked the older man on sight, and things did not improve.

"Need to talk to you, Harvey."

"About what?" He looked as if he barely knew me. I turned to the seated man, whose eyes had never left me.

"You done? I need to talk to Harvey."

"Siddown, Frank. Nothing you need to hide from me." He winked at Harvey. "After all, you and me are practically partners." I didn't sit down.

"Bob here is one of our investigators, Frank. You know, one with a license? He was looking into the Gonzalez file when you decided to do more than we asked you to."

"Don't think we don't appreciate it, Frank, but you've got a funny idea about what a background checker does. Good thing you don't know what you're doing, or you might have messed me up. Maybe even gone to the school where the dead guy spent ninety percent of his waking hours."

It didn't take a degree in physics to see what had happened. They'd given me the basic stuff while assigning an actual PI to do the real digging. While I'd been hanging around at the library and interviewing the dead boy's father, this Bob character had been asking questions at Farragut. Harvey should have told me about him, if only to keep me from getting in his way, but then again it was unlikely that our paths would have crossed. Just looking at him, I suspected this particular PI couldn't type his own name on a PC and that he was hated by every court clerk this side of the Mississippi.

"So you're the guy who said Gonzalez was involved in gambling."

"Only reporting what I heard. But I heard it enough times to know it's true."

"Even if you did, what difference does it make? Why is the policy on hold?"

"Criminal activity negates that policy, Frank." Harvey spoke archly, as if he were explaining that high treason is a death penalty offense.

"Are you saying he was killed for gambling debts?" I turned to the smiling Bob. "Do you even know if he was ahead or behind?"

"I don't have to, and it's all thanks to you. A young man just doesn't buy life insurance, Frank, even if he thinks he could be killed at any moment. A guy who doesn't value his life enough to avoid this kind of danger sure doesn't care about someone else getting money when he's finally gone. So no, the gambling alone isn't enough. But then you brought me the missing piece."

"The baby."

"The baby." Harvey was in insurance heaven. "You see, Frank, the insurance game isn't as straightforward as people think it is. Sometimes it takes a little digging, a little connect-the-dots, but when you have a hidden lifestyle and a motive, you've got someone trying to commit insurance fraud."

"Or a reason to deny a claim."

"Same thing." He reached into his desk and came up with an envelope. "Here's your fee. One-fifty as agreed. Looks like you could use it."

Bob was still smirking at me as I numbly reached out and took it. I had passed into that netherworld where you know the people you're confronting are lying to you, or that their motives are one-hundred-eighty degrees off of what they say they are, but for some reason I couldn't find a crack in what they'd said.

"Tell me one thing, Harvey. Why does everyone, and I mean everyone, think I came up with this gambling excuse?"

"Hey, you're the one who decided to go and talk to Dannon and Gonzalez. Heck, right now you're more the public face of Sun Provident than I am. I haven't given your name to anybody."

"Any idea where Michael Escobar works?"

"Sure, Tanner and Briscoe over in Davis." He stopped suddenly, seeing that he'd just revealed his phone conversation with the Michael Escobar who now wanted to put me in intensive care. "We do business with them all the time."

"Thanks, Harv." I held up the envelope. "This is my severance. From now on, just use Bob here for everything, including the face-to-face stuff with the relatives."

They were both laughing fraternally when I walked out, as if I needed time to cool off and would realize we were all buddies once enough time had passed. I left the nail where it was.

As a note in passing, never argue with two people at once. If you start to pin one of them down, the other can jump in and save him. Even so, I had managed to get an important piece of information from Harvey and, combining that with Michael Escobar's phone message, come to a pretty solid conclusion: No matter who was trying to run me off, Michael Escobar had not put the bullet on my kitchen table.

I drove up the highway to get to Davis, passing acres and acres of the Panhandle's ubiquitous longleaf pines. The tall trees with their tendril-like needles seemed to bore most of the people who lived around me, but I liked them. They didn't allow a lot of secondary growth beneath them, and seemed spaced just far enough apart to suggest that I park my car and simply go for a walk. The trees were resistant to fire and many of the deadlier parasitic insects in the region, and I felt a survivor's kinship with them.

All too soon I pulled into the booming metropolis of Davis and wondered for the hundredth time if this was what was in store for Exile and other small towns farther down the coast. I hoped not, even if Davis did provide me with a little taste of city living from time to time when I got homesick.

Directory assistance had given me the address for Tanner & Briscoe, Attorneys-at-Law, and I was a little surprised that they had their offices in a modest two-story building near the old center of town instead of in one of the new high-rises. I had to figure that they already had a well-established practice, didn't need help from new and impressive digs, and understood that fixed costs have to be met whether you have clients or not. I'd found that out the hard way and respected people who kept the monthly nut small.

I used a side door to get inside and found myself in a large open floor where a dozen paralegals, administrative assistants, and other support people were seated in a colony of small cubicles. The cubes were those insane waist-high playpens that allow the entire floor to see what you are doing and encourage people on either side of you to talk to each other through one side of your head and out the other. I picked out a young man with dark hair, probably twenty-five, who looked like the type who would leave threats of violence on someone's answering machine. I approached him from behind, but it wasn't necessary because he had on a set of headphones and was typing madly into the keyboard in front of him. A name tag on the cube wall identified him as Michael Escobar, and I took a deep breath before tapping him on the shoulder.

He seemed pleased when he turned around, and as soon as the earphones were gone he spoke.

"Mr. Cole. I hope you've got some good news for me."

Michael Escobar was a good-looking guy, very Latin, with a set of big teeth that flashed pure white. Paralegal or no, he recognized me immediately, and so I had to figure he'd done quite a bit of homework on me.

"Can we go outside?"

"Even better. I can't give you credit for brains, *hermano,* but you've got some *huevos.* We'll see if you've still got them when we're done."

"Go easy on the Hispanic gangbanger stuff, will ya?" I asked with genuine annoyance. I pointed a finger at his necktie and short-sleeved white shirt. "It doesn't fit. And if you start swinging before you hear me out, you'll never straighten out that insurance claim."

I turned my back on him and walked out the way I came in. He didn't follow too quickly, so it was possible that I'd get in a few words before having to run as fast as I could. When I turned around he was standing in the doorway, flicking a lighter under a cigarette and looking unconcerned. I still figured him to punch me at least once, but maybe the uncle of an unborn child with no father is entitled to hit the guy he thinks is trashing his family.

"It's not the money, Mr. Cole." He started before I could speak, his words flowing in a deep singsong. He took the cigarette out and regarded me with derision. "You really are a lousy investigator, aren't you? My dad's got real estate all up and down the Gulf. We don't need the money.

"What I want to know is, why did you go making poor Rosie Gonzalez think you're an okay guy when you were out to smear his son?"

"Maybe you won't believe me, but the truth is I was just handling the paperwork on this case and there was another investigator, a real PI, who was . . . digging for dirt."

The cigarette went back in his mouth while he mockingly clapped his hands.

"Good try, mister. You think we don't hear stuff like that right here in the office? 'It wasn't me, counselor, it was this other guy!' " He shook his head as if I were boring him, and I started to come to the conclusion that Michael Escobar was smarter than he acted.

"I can get you a name if you want. He's a forty-something private investigator, red face, said he works for Sun Provident a lot, first name's Bob."

"Bob Barstow? I've seen him here in the office a couple of times. Even the lawyers don't like him." He looked like he was chewing on this for a moment. "Okay, maybe. That fits Barstow and those Sun Provident guys, but so what? You're with them. Why did you come around here?"

"Two reasons. One, in your phone message you didn't accuse me of lying. Even now you still haven't said that Eddie wasn't into gambling."

He looked at me sideways, and I wasn't sure if this was an

unconscious self-rebuke for letting that slip or the suspicion that I was digging for even more bad news on his formerly prospective brother-in-law.

"You said two. What's the other reason?"

"Two days ago I got a little visit from some professional people who broke into my place. No sign of forced entry except a little message trying to scare me away from the Eddie Gonzalez case. So far you're the only guy who's threatened me since that happened."

"So?"

"In my book that means you weren't the one who left me the message."

He didn't shake my hand when I left, but he hadn't punched me either. He'd spent a lot of time around Rosie Gonzalez growing up and obviously thought the world of the man. It made me wonder just how much of his acceptance of my story was based on an earnest belief that Rosie was a good judge of people. In both the legal and the investigative world it's important to identify people around you who can size someone up quickly, particularly if you're not good at it yourself, and I had to think he viewed Rosie in that light.

The information he gave me saved me a trip out to Farragut, which was good because I needed to go back inside my hole at this point. Eddie had indeed been putting some money down on sports gambling. Apparently it's all over every campus in America now, but according to Escobar it was all chump change. He maintained that Eddie had always exhibited a bit of an inferiority complex around the Escobars' relative affluence, but the effect had been to spur the gas station owner's son to work like a madman at getting a degree while painting houses all summer. As it turned out, he and Eddie had been friends at Exile High together, and that was how Eddie had met Anneliese, not the other way around.

If Eddie were the focus of my troubles I would have had to dig deeper than that, but as far as I was concerned he wasn't. There were people trying to discourage me from taking a good hard look at what had happened on that jogging path, and so far no one in the picture, from the dead guy to the beneficiaries, fit that mold.

So back to the tapes. I had been looking over my shoulder the entire length of my trip from Harvey's office to Davis, and I really began watching as I got closer to Bending Palms. This paranoia started to look like it would pay off right about then, as there had been a tan car, looked like a four-door, a few vehicles back ever since I left Escobar. There were two white male faces in the front seat, and they turned onto the two-lane highway with the longleaf pines when I did.

It was midafternoon and the highway had a steady flow of cars on it, not busy but never empty, and so I felt reasonably safe in checking these guys. It was important to pick a stretch of road where they couldn't suddenly turn off behind me, as I needed them to go by. Once I found a good expanse of nothing but trees I simply pulled over. The tan car didn't miss a beat, going by as if nothing were wrong, and the guys inside didn't do anything silly like pretending to sneeze just as they passed me. The one on the passenger side was big enough to block my view of the driver just by sitting up straight, but I got a good look at him. Sandy blond hair, a lantern jaw, brown suit. I got the license plate as they continued up the road, but something told me it would turn out to be a rental.

And I sure as heck didn't try to follow them.

Back in Todd Stanley's dark little room, I found him going over the tapes and could have kissed him. Somewhere in the previous two days he had come to the conclusion that his new friend the rumpled insurance investigator was not doing municipal bond work, but he'd taken a liking to me and obviously loved his surveillance cameras. He'd also noticed that when I went on a food run I bought all three of the day's meals at once and that my choices had been limited. There was a steak sandwich, fries, and a soda waiting for me, so I dropped the act and let him in on what I was doing.

He liked it even better than the story about getting the jogging trail closed. Real PI work, possibly even a murder, and using his footage, no less. In no time at all he was identifying some of the faces that were on the trail every night sometime around sunset, also pointing out the ones that he'd never seen before, and finally asking what Eddie Gonzalez had actually looked like.

I popped in one of the tapes from a condo complex closer to Exile, one that showed the kid when he was still alive. Although the film at Todd's compound went back to before the accident, Eddie had never appeared in any of that footage, not even after I had calculated how long it would have taken him to get there from the other condo's camera. It seemed a safe assumption that he turned around before getting there. He'd appeared twice in front of that other compound's camera in the two days prior to the incident, and it had been a sad and eerie thing to watch him jog by on the night it happened. He'd been tall and lean, already tanned from the house painting, and moving with that floating ease that marks the real runners.

Todd scrunched forward on his chair when I stilled the movement for him. He looked at Eddie in the orange front-and-back jogging vest and its horizontal reflector striping with the fascination of a man seeing a ghost. Which was exactly what he was seeing.

"Frank, when you were looking at my tapes, did you check any of the ones that were shot before the accident?"

"Well, I did look at the coverage two days before it happened, but I've been mostly focused on the ones since then. Why?"

"Guy must be outta town," he mumbled as he went to the small cabinet where he kept the recordings. He reused the same cartridges over and over, so there weren't that many of them, and he quickly found the one he was looking for. He popped it in and began fast-forwarding to the right time frame. "Here we go. This is the oldest one I have, three nights before the accident."

The now-familiar sight of the back parking lot came into focus, with a few cars and a Dumpster showing up in the gray twilight world. The lights in the parking lot blazed down on the far edge, where the fitness trail actually ended briefly and the path's users walked right across the hot top. It was just getting dark at this point in the film, and there were only a few people biking or walking past the camera. A teenager skateboarding where he shouldn't have been flat-wheeled his way through.

And then a man who looked quite a bit like Eddie ran through, going toward Exile many miles away. Though obviously much older, he ran easily enough, his black hair bouncing slightly and his muscled arms swinging on either side of the jogging vest he wore. The parking lot lights bounced off of the reflector strips, and then he was gone.

"I knew I'd seen him before. He's not your boy, but he goes by here pretty regularly, right about the same time of night."

"But he hasn't been on any of the tapes since it happened. I wonder where he's been."

"And who he is."

CHAPTER FOUR

The price of Todd's invaluable assistance came that night, while we were cataloging the various times when the Eddie Gonzalez look-alike commonly crossed the parking lot. I'd already told him that I was hiding from some people who didn't want me looking into this case, but while we were jawing he asked me why I didn't have any help.

There was no reason to tell him the story, but I'd spilled the beans to Gray Toliver a few days before and it seemed as if enough time had passed where I could discuss it with strangers. Besides, he'd been a good sport about the white lie I'd originally told him, and I wasn't going to push that any farther.

"Well, Todd, a year ago I was winding up the bankruptcy of a software company I used to own. It was up north in Connecticut, close to New York City, and I'd had the business for six years . . ."

And as bad as the last three were, I wouldn't trade the first three for anything in the world. I'd spent the first year scared to death, working twenty-hour days because I was too worried to sleep. If you're wondering what bothered me so much, let me tell you there is nothing quite like the feeling of signing papers where a bank gives you five hundred thousand dollars and you see just how much of that you have to give back every month.

Every single month, rain or shine, business or no business. If that's not tough enough, add in the rent on the office space (nothing fancy there; the key is to keep the overhead low), the lease money on the furniture and office machines, and the payroll. There are other monthly fixed costs, but I think you get the idea. In a normal business you can use this method to calculate your breakeven, the amount of revenue you need to meet your obligations, but in my work it doesn't quite go that way.

In addition to running the day-to-day office affairs, we were tailoring basic business software to meet the specific needs of a wide variety of clients. Even though that was tough, it beat the heck out of having no clients at all, and so we were happy for the work. The trick was billing enough while still in development to fund the remaining phases of each project, and we had some scary financial moments in the first months, but by the end of the first year I pretty much got the hang of it. One day I woke up wondering where the sick dread of so many previous mornings had gone, and it was then that I realized I had gotten some kind of handle on the tiger I was riding.

We began to show a nice healthy profit at the end of the second year, and that was when I simply had to lay on some extra bodies. We still worked out of the same small office space, but there was a lot more time on the road between the new clients' installations and the old clients' upkeep. The whole thing clicked and whirred nicely, and by the end of the third year we'd even been written up in a couple of magazines. I still had a picture from the first (and only) company picnic, upward of fifty people all waving and smiling into the camera on an impossibly sunny day at the beach. Just looking at that photo could bring back the feeling of those days, the belief that we had fought just hard enough to win ourselves a future.

That was when a modest recession hit. Even though we were well into the fourth year when the numbers began getting soft, the clients began dropping their plans for upgrades almost immediately. We still had plenty of work in the pipeline, and the accountants kept telling me we were all right, but every night I sat there transfixed by the financial news on the television, listening for and never hearing that the worst was over. Somewhere in the fourth year the first cancellations came in, and you could say that was when I made a mistake.

In the long run it would have made little difference, but as the cancellations started, I graciously let every one of our clients off the hook. I was so sure that the economy was just about to turn the corner, and I figured that the clients would come back if we treated them well when things were rough. Many of them owed us money. There were penalties for calling off a project once it was past a certain point, and I could have really put the screws to them if I had wanted to. The sad truth was that most of my clients were small to midrange companies like mine, and in the desperate eyes of the other owners I saw my own mounting fear.

My creditors got a lot of mileage out of that decision when it came time to file for bankruptcy protection. In the meantime I started missing payments a lot sooner than I would have if I had simply been tough, and so I did the two things you really shouldn't do. First, I plowed my own money in, which was a tidy pile at the start and a big fat zero a few quick months later. Second, I arranged for what the financiers call "expensive money." While in no way illegal, this is a mezzanine level of funding that business owners go to when the bankers won't even return their calls anymore. It comes in many forms, but the basic version is a pool of money from some fat cats looking to make a thick percentage in a short-term situation or to scoop up a failing asset at fire-sale prices.

My company had been the latter. In the course of our twenty-hour days we'd developed a good name and a couple of nifty innovations on which we held the patents. Yes, I know, what's a patent in the software business, but even when competitors reverse-engineer your stuff, they prefer to do it legally. Getting hold of the patents is a good way to get legal, and the fat cats behind my expensive financing already had the sale of our rights in mind when they cut us the first check.

The recession ended a few weeks after we were forced into selling the company off. By then I was a total wreck, feeling like someone who has nursed a sick loved one for years only to see her die in the end. It was only my friend Mark who kept the patents out of the hands of the other side. They ended up in a legal limbo, not mine and not the fat-cat financiers', and near as I can tell they still sit in a drawer in an insurance office that had to pay out some pretty hefty penalties for my decisions.

That wasn't the worst part, though. Losing the business hurt, and the feeling that I had dropped so many years into something that had failed hurt even more, but it was the employees' hurt that really got to me. I've been using the pronoun "we" a lot here, and I mean it. I had the greatest set of people working in that company, from the office manager who kept everything straight to the programmers who sometimes slept at their desks. Letting them go one by one was like deciding which family heirloom to sell, and even though most of them understood, some of them didn't. My failure to collect money owed to us was common knowledge by then, and I heard about it more than once when giving the bad news to another one of my people.

That was what Michael Escobar had been talking about in his phone message. No one seemed to know that I lost everything when that company died, but they sure seemed to know it was my fault.

And the words of the dotty judge who decided to punish me as a lesson to corporate America by attaching my future earnings were just a whisper compared to what some of my own people said to me.

"Wow." Todd wasn't even looking at the tape when I came out of my reverie. "I don't mean to make you feel any worse here, Frank, but I gotta say that I have never even *heard* of somebody getting run over that bad. And up to now I thought I'd heard everything."

Well, that wasn't so bad, really. Telling, I mean. Both Todd and Gray had been sympathetic, and in a way it helped that two strangers, totally removed from the story, saw me as at least partially blameless. It was possible that they were just being nice, too, but I chose not to see it that way.

In the meantime I now had a very good photograph of the man who might just have been the intended victim on the night Eddie Gonzalez perished. The folks at the video store had printed me several copies, but now I was faced with a true quandary in that this was all I had. Todd did not know who the man in the photo was, and he had not appeared in any of the video footage since the night of the event. Even though it would have been better to have him available on the fitness trail, perhaps it wasn't such a bad thing that I could not physically approach him yet. After all, I believed someone had tried to run him over just two weeks before and had no idea if he might be someone who actually deserved it.

There was also the distinct possibility that he had fallen victim to his enemies since then. That would explain his absence from the jogging path where Todd said he was almost a nightly fixture. Add in the shadowy figures who had threatened me and then tailed me, and it was certainly a moment for sober thought. I wondered if scanning the local obituaries might yield his name, but there was no guarantee he was dead or that a death notice would contain enough information for me to use. His would-be assassins' efforts to make the original crime look like an accident suggested that they weren't likely to do the same thing in the same vicinity, particularly if an investigator for the insurance company might see the description of the second crime in the newspaper.

And even though he might be dead, there was just as much chance that his enemies had been forced to reconsider their plan and that I was playing with his life by moving slowly. I finally decided that discretion was the better part of valor for the time being, and that knowing who he was might at least indicate if he were a dangerous hoodlum or simply an intended murder victim who was still alive. It might also provide me with a phone number that I could use to contact him, which would probably be safer for the both of us.

There was certainly some evidence to go on. The reflector vest and hair color were not the only things that might have caused Eddie Gonzalez to be mistaken for this man, if that was what had happened. I estimated the man's age at forty-five, but he ran like a twenty-year-old. Add in the tinted glass and the darkness, and the tragic case of mistaken identity fit pretty well. Not that I could take any of that to the police, mind you, but it sure looked solid to me.

I had to think a guy that age who ran that much and that well probably competed in quite a few road races, maybe triathlons or even an ironman. On the film he came from the direction of West Bending Palms, turned around somewhere, and came back on through. Although he looked fit enough to have come all the way from Mobile, all of this suggested that he lived to the west, and so I took the picture and headed out to the running stores.

It had been three days since I had been home, and I was now so sick of hiding that a possible run-in with my anonymous playmates did not frighten me enough to keep me off the scent. Luckily I was headed toward the tony part of our little Panhandle neighborhood, the wealthy enclave of Davis, and there was very little chance they would do something right there in the business district. As a parting gesture Todd had let me wash my clothes and sleep in the shed, so I was both rested and presentable when I set off the next morning.

Identifying the unknown jogger by showing his picture to other runners was a long shot. I had already surmised that he might not buy his shoes at any of the local sporting goods stores, but I still believed that the people who managed those places would recognize him from various races. I avoided the one-size-fits-all sports shops and hit only the ones specializing in running gear, and at the third one I hit pay dirt.

Dressed as I was in the light suit jacket with the tie, I did not fit the part of a racehorse asking about the local champion, so instead I colored the truth just a bit. At each place I showed the photo as I walked up, said I was reporting on the local talent, and asked if they recognized the man in the print. It was actually close to the truth, because I was certainly hoping to write some kind of report on this man. If I were going to get Sun Provident to honor its insurance policy I was going to have to demonstrate conclusively that Eddie Gonzalez's gambling activities had not led to his demise. That would require a detailed report involving this man, and if the guy behind the counter at the running store thought he heard me say I was a journalist, I can assure you he did not.

The third store was a small affair jammed with running shoes, shorts, tape, canteens, electronic mileage gauges, tank tops, tube tops, athletic bras, and a whole bunch of other equipment I did not recognize. The guy behind the counter was thin as a rail, tanned like a saddle, and wore his gray hair pulled back in a ponytail. As I walked up I just knew he was tuned in to every major running event in the area going back decades, which was a relief, because the last place had been more of a jogging boutique than a serious racer's supply center. I flashed the picture at the bone-hard eyes behind the cash register.

"Hi, I'm doing a little reporting on the local running scene and saw this guy eating up the road the other night. He looked pretty fast for a guy his age, too fast for me anyway, but I still wanted to interview him. Do you recognize him?" I was ready to hand the print over, but that turned out to be unnecessary.

"Sure do. You one of those reporters who only read the sports section?"

"I beg your pardon?"

"You should talk to the folks who write the business section. That's Drew Spector." He stared at me as if waiting for the lightbulb to go on over my head. "Drew Spector. You know, the CEO of Hayward Shipping."

One of the tough things about being a transplant is that the locals sometimes assume you know everything they do. I had only been in the Panhandle for nine months, and much of that had been spent adjusting to my new status as a guy trying not to earn any money, so I must admit I was not familiar with the local news.

"So he's a pretty well-known guy around here? Runs races, I mean?"

The ponytail guy seemed to lose interest in me at that moment, reaching down for a deck of running chronometers that sat in the glass front of the checkout. I must have interrupted him when he was cleaning, because he removed the gadgets and stacked them on a low shelf behind him while he talked.

"I don't think I've ever seen him race, actually. Didn't even know he was a runner. But if he is, his training schedule is probably all blown to there and gone by now, what with selling the company and all."

I wanted to strangle him. Somewhere in that carrot-eating carcass was some very relevant information, and yet he seemed more interested in Windexing the display case than answering my questions. I pulled out a notebook and jotted down the names Drew Spector and Hayward Shipping, figuring that some more time on the Internet might be in order. On a hunch I asked one last question.

"Anybody around here unhappy about that?"

"About what?"

"This Spector, selling the company. And all."

"Not many, if you don't count the union, the employees, and all the businesses up and down the coast that are gonna go belly-up when the layoffs start."

I leaned back in one of the chairs at the Exile town library. I'd parked the car several blocks away and entered the building through the loading entrance, straight into the librarians' office area. Mary Beth had taken pity on me when I asked to use her computer to log on to the Web, or maybe she had sensed that I was trying not to be seen and didn't want me to be seen either, and so I was not out in public view. Her PC had all the extras that the reference area machines had, and in no time at all I had a working knowledge of the life of Drew Spector.

He was a public guy, to say the least.

Fifty years old, he looked ten years younger than that. I had to wonder if it was the running I had witnessed or the charmed life he seemed to lead. In a nutshell, Drew Spector lived a life of accomplishment. He was the current CEO of Hayward Shipping, a small but extremely well-run freight-hauling enterprise working the Gulf of Mexico and the Caribbean. Hayward had ships all over the Gulf Coast and much of Central America, warehouses and dock facilities, and a spotless reputation in the trade.

Spector himself mirrored this. Born into a Charleston money family, he had a bachelor's degree in economics from Harvard and a graduate degree in finance from the University of Edinburgh. His business biography listed a string of struggling or failing companies which he had turned around over the years, each one bigger than the last, until this became his standard identifier. He was now a professional chief executive officer, getting hired for obscene amounts of money to improve the bottom line at various ailing corporations.

That last bit gave me pause. Hayward Shipping was certainly big enough for him, and a man like Spector would probably view this unfamiliar freight-hauling business as a challenge, but Hayward was not in any kind of trouble. I punched up its basic financials and reviewed the business news prior to its sale, and nothing seemed out of place. The shipping company's overall health was good enough that they were even referring to its sale as a merger. That terminology might just have been an accounting trick, but Hayward was certainly being bought, and you really can't call it a merger if the target is a financial cripple. Everything I read told me that Hayward Shipping was a very well-run company that had simply been snapped up by a bigger fish, and I wondered why a turnaround guy had been put in charge of it in the first place.

Well, making a mountain out of a molehill is one of the hazards of the fact-checking business, and I had caught myself doing this kind of thing before. I had to wonder if my previous life as a business owner made me review the financial side of investigations with extra zeal, and so in this case I made myself move on. Even if Hayward was a good outfit, directorial boards are always looking to improve revenues and it wouldn't be the first time that a turnaround expert was brought in to fix something that wasn't broken.

But that was where they'd made a mistake, judging from the vituperation of the editorials running up and down the coast. There was ten times as much coverage after the announcement of the merger as before, and I got a sinking feeling when I saw just how many people disliked Mr. Drew Spector.

"Gone from a real victim without an enemy in the world to an intended victim hated by everyone who knows him," I muttered as I looked at one of the many pictures of Spector. Here was Spector in a sober business suit, sitting at the head of a large conference table, his chair pushed back so that one leg could be crossed over the other. Here was another shot with the tall, athletic man piloting some kind of racing vessel, wind in his full hair and features twisted with enjoyment. Here was another showing Spector with an attractive woman who was obviously his wife and two impossibly beautiful children.

The write-ups in the business magazines all fawned over him as the Second Coming, but the local news was much different. Everyone from union leaders to shopkeepers opposed the sale of Hayward, even though it was not apparent that the merger was going to mean big changes in the area. After all, the analysts pointed out, the acquiring corporation owned nothing north of the equator and so there was presumably little redundancy to be chopped out.

That didn't seem to satisfy his own board, however, as there had apparently been quite a split of opinion over the sale. According to the chief financial officer, an aged gentleman named Sanford Hurst who had been with Hayward for forty years, Spector had gone out and lined up the sale without consulting a single member of the board. Hurst was described as a local millionaire, the scion of a family that had helped found Hayward generations before, and Spector's predecessor as CEO. Apparently Hurst had decided to step down from the top spot and had recruited Spector personally.

The sale had been authorized by a four-to-three vote, and it sounded like Hurst was wrong about how much Spector had discussed the transaction with the board. Hayward had been a pretty insular company before Spector took the helm, and he had apparently expanded the board in the name of good corporate governance. He had brought three outsiders with him, and those three new directors were no doubt in lockstep with his plan. Their votes alone weren't quite enough to approve the merger, though, and one of the older set must have switched sides to give them the fourth and deciding ballot.

You could practically hear the whispered promises in the back rooms and the clubs, the offering behind the scenes of power and riches.

"Bet that didn't make him popular with Mr. Hurst," I thought as I continued to read. "Probably another guy who should start looking both ways before crossing the street."

Unfortunately, the vocal Mr. Hurst had not named the turncoat. I had to go through three different articles about the sale before learning why this salient piece of information was not common knowledge. According to one local paper, the Hayward board always kept its deliberations secret and would not reveal the details about the vote other than to publish the results. I suppose a good stockholder lawsuit could force them to say who had voted which way, but if the tally had been a secret ballot that would not work.

I was paying close attention to the dates involved here, and the announcement of the merger had been just two weeks ago, three days after Eddie Gonzalez's death. Spector had gone to a meeting in Caracas the morning after the accident, unknowingly putting himself out of harm's way, and he'd only returned a week ago. That was why he hadn't been on the surveillance tapes in the days just after the incident.

It left an interesting question. Even if the killers had hit Eddie by accident, why hadn't they tried again during the intervening weeks? The local law had written off Eddie's demise as a hit-and-run by teen car thieves, just as they'd been meant to, so what was stopping the would-be assassins from getting rid of Spector now? With all of the people who hated him, there might not even be a need to make it look like an accident. And now that I knew the man on the jogging trail was not some dangerous criminal, I was probably obligated to inform him of his peril.

I took a few moments to do something I should have done earlier, and called Rosie Gonzalez. I wanted to let him know that I had not been the one responsible for getting the insurance claim flagged. As it turned out, he had already spoken to Mike Escobar.

"Well, thanks for calling me back, Mr. Cole." He sounded wary on the phone, and I had to think that he was never going to trust me again. "Mike told me you went to see him, so I suppose that shows I wasn't completely wrong about you. I was just very surprised to hear that someone would go to these lengths to deny an insurance claim."

"Mr. Gonzalez, I assure you I had nothing to do with getting that claim flagged. When I left Sun Provident's offices I was convinced that they were going to make good. And then . . . Well, I got sidetracked a little right after that."

"Michael told me you were threatened. Again I have to say that I can't imagine how that could be related to my family, or the Escobars."

"It's not, Mr. Gonzalez. I can't give you much more information than that right now, but I am almost certain that there is a whole other group of people involved here. And they had nothing to do with your son."

"Except maybe they killed him?"

At the best of times I'm no good with basic interviews, but under the circumstances I just didn't know what to say. I cleared my throat.

"That is very possible, sir. But I have to keep looking to know for sure."

"Mr. Cole, I don't know you very well, but I have to caution you if these people threatened you. There's already been a life senselessly lost. Maybe you should drop this."

It crossed my mind that Rosie didn't have much faith in my abilities as an investigator, but I decided to take him at his word and accepted his advice as simple concern from a grieving father. Before I could answer he called out something in Spanish to someone nearby, and then he was back on.

"Mr. Cole, Anneliese is here. She just walked in and I think she has something to say to you."

Well, my luck was certainly continuing true to form. What were the odds that Anneliese Escobar would drop in at Gonzalez Auto and Gas just as I was patching things up with the preternaturally reasonable Rosie? Of all the people in this case, the very last one I wanted to talk to was the dead man's fiancée, but Gonzalez handed off the phone with a muted flurry of Spanish. If Mike Escobar's hostile reaction was any measure, I was about to get my head taken off.

"Mr. Cole?" The voice on the other end was feminine and uncertain.

"Yes, Miss Escobar, this is Frank Cole."

"How could you, Mr. Cole?" The voice was small and accusing. "How *could* you?"

And the line went dead. In retrospect, getting my head taken off would have been a lot less painful.

It was getting late when Mary Beth chased me away from her PC, and about the only thing I knew for sure at that point was that I needed help with this. For a fact-checker I'd done a pretty good job, but this convoluted knot required a professional to unravel. Or at least someone licensed to ask the kind of questions I needed answered. Someone smooth enough to get an interview with Mr. Drew Spector, business magnate, turnaround king, and the most hated man in Florida.

Mary Beth was good enough to let me use her phone, and I dialed the number of my mentor, William Haskell, of Haskell Private Investigations.

CHAPTER FIVE

When I say Bill Haskell is my mentor, I am referring to the time frame since I came down to Florida and got into the periphery of the private investigations industry. I am also speaking pretty much tongue in cheek, as Haskell easily got as much from our relationship as I did.

My buddy Mark's game plan of keeping my earnings low would have been easy to follow in the private investigations business even if I had been working like a dog. I think I already said that PIs have to really put in the hours to turn a profit, and so my lackadaisical efforts had certainly kept me close to the poverty line. While that no doubt maddened my creditors and confounded my dotty judge, it didn't leave me much in the way of pocket change. Basically operating on a budget, I had become quite adept at getting things for free. It is amazing what is out there if you just apply yourself.

Instead of a gym membership I had the Exile recreation center. Instead of my own PC at home I had the library reference section. Instead of clubbing it, I had Gray Toliver's diabolical chess play, and instead of wealthy investors I had the Small Business Administration.

Hey, don't knock it, particularly if you're thinking of starting your own business. There are thousands of civil servants being paid to help the low-level entrepreneur, all for free, and it is amazing what you can get from them. In fact, that is where I got Bill Haskell. He was part of the SBA's mentoring program, which links up experienced business people with starry-eyed small business owners. Having been around the track a few hundred times, these folks know everything from the proper writing of a business plan to the accurate calculation of a breakeven point.

If I had availed myself of this service in my software company, it is highly likely that one of those people would have told me to collect everything owed to me when things got tough. Even if it would not have staved off ruin, it might have made me look like a much better manager when the bankruptcy started. In case I didn't mention this earlier, my bad decisions allowed my creditors to force my business into liquidation instead of a reorganization.

At any rate, most of the mentors in this program are retired business people, and very few of them come from the realm of private investigations. Not down in my neck of the woods, anyway. At forty, Bill Haskell was far from retirement, and I swear he put his name on the SBA list as part of a never-ending quest to network with the entire world.

Bill owned his own agency and employed three men and two women in addition to a modest office staff. He had been in the business since he was a teenager, when he had gotten his start in repossessions. It was rumored that he started repossessing cars before he was licensed to drive, and ten minutes into our first meeting I believed every word of it.

In my opinion, Bill was a little on the shady side. He had that unusual ability to be all things to all men, and he could make himself fit in at a longshoreman's bar or a dress cotillion. He had heard of the SBA's mentor program and had signed on as a means of identifying new talent and extending his network of business contacts, not to mention getting favorable consideration from the government for being a volunteer. I doubted he viewed me as a new talent, but he had offered to sign me on to his firm several times. I was required more than once to tell him I wasn't looking to make a pile of money.

He seemed to know everybody, and I don't mean he was a name-dropper. One time we met at a nice restaurant near his office in Tallahassee, and at that meeting he was in more of the dress cotillion mode than the longshoreman's bar mode. The place was packed with the political movers of Florida state politics, at least the ones up north anyway, and we barely got through a sentence or a serving without another lawyer or politician coming up to shake his hand. He also jumped up out of his seat to greet some of the bigger names that came across the floor, and I had to admire the effort he put into pressing the flesh.

Bill once said that he never turned down a case and never betrayed a trust, intimating that those two rules were the secret of his success. I have since had occasion to question some of the things he has told me, but the grateful expressions on some of the faces in that restaurant suggested that Bill Haskell had the reputation of a man who gets the job done and then forgets it ever happened.

Under the current circumstances, and considering the weight of the people involved, I was pretty happy to be able to turn to him. He happened to be at the office when I called, which was unusual in that Haskell loved detective work and was always out and about supervising his people or investigating something on his own. As the party who wanted to see him, I applied my own rule of meeting protocol and offered to drive to Tallahassee the next day. I was not able to give much detail over the phone, but he was either intrigued or bored enough to suggest we meet that night.

I walked into the Gator Pond bar just after nine and saw that Bill was back in longshoreman mode. That was fitting, as the Gator Pond was nothing more than a dive. Haskell was seated at the bar, engaged in a raucous discussion with several drunken lowlifes and looking like a man having a good time. He was dressed in a set of light-colored jeans and a white T-shirt that advertised an air show from a few years before. The place was packed, with a long bar down the left-hand side and a few small tables off to the right. Country music blasted from the jukebox, and I hoped we wouldn't be staying.

As I got closer I was able to make out Haskell's shouted words.

"—turns out this wheelchair guy was a navy man—"

"This part of the country, what else?" shouted one of the lowlifes, hanging on every word.

"—a navy man, stood deck watches all over the world, and now that he's a shut-in, he does the same thing. Sits at his window all day every day, binoculars in hand, and, no joke, logs every license plate that goes by."

Haskell had them eating out of his hand. They obviously knew he was a PI, and I must have missed an important piece of information by coming in on the story late, because the four guys around him felt that the logging of the license plates was significant. They variously "oohed" and "ahhed," and one of them even slapped the bar a time or two.

"So, obviously I've got what I need, got this cheatin' husband dead to rights, but it turns out the lady in question was pretty popular—"

The listeners interjected their own suppositions about the lady's physical characteristics and mating habits, and Haskell waited until they subsided.

"—and so, being a professional and just a thorough guy all around, I thought it might be a good idea to run that entire list of plates and find out who these other gentlemen callers were. I mean, if this went to divorce court the lawyers might want to subpoena them as character witnesses."

"Who'd you catch, Bill? Who'd ya catch?"

"Now, you know I cannot divulge any of the information I obtain while working a case"—a chorus of "noooo's" and "nevers" followed this—"but let's just say I haven't gotten a parking ticket in this county in quite . . . some . . . time."

He tilted his head to signify the end of the story, wearing a grin that was half smugness and half levity. While the listeners were laughing he flipped a bill onto the bar, made a circle with his finger to let the bartender know that he was buying a round, and slipped out of the middle of the group. He reached out an arm to me, dropped a hand on my shoulder, and steered me easily through a crowd of toughs and scumbags that I would have run away from under any other circumstance.

There was a door near the jukebox, and he produced a key to open it. I shook my head in admiration as we went through the door into a quiet back room that was just big enough for several stacked cases of beer and a table with chairs.

"So what's on your mind, Frank?" he asked as he lit up a cigarette and dropped into one of the chairs. He was only medium height, but well built, with a head of red curls starting to go gray.

I told him. He interrupted me when I mentioned the bullet on the kitchen table, just to ask if I had any other open cases going when that happened. When I explained that the bullet was sitting on a newspaper clipping describing Eddie Gonzalez's accident, he made an observation without taking the smoke out of his mouth. "They were thinking the same thing I was. They wanted to make sure you didn't confuse their warning with another case."

I went on, keeping to chronological order. He interrupted again when I described the car that had tailed me from the meeting with Mike Escobar.

"You sure these guys weren't on you when you left Exile?"

"Absolutely. I've grown eyes in the back of my head ever since seeing that bullet."

"So they picked you up at the law firm where Escobar works."

"Right."

He told me to go on, and didn't interrupt again even as I described the tedious review of the surveillance footage and my reasons for believing the accident might actually have been an attempted murder.

"So the guy in the film turns out to be an individual named Drew Spector, CEO of—"

It was all I could have hoped for. As much as Haskell seemed to like me and enjoyed dispensing his PI wisdom, I doubted very strongly that he would take time to help out with a case unless there was a potential for big money or some new link in his network. Drew Spector was both.

"Drew Spector!" he burst out, placing emphasis on each word. His face lit up and he got a crazy, avaricious gleam in his eye. "That's one mighty big elephant, boy. And none too popular these days, either. You haven't tried to contact him, have you?"

"No. I called you as soon as I identified him."

"Good. He's way out of your league, probably wouldn't see you even if you convinced him his life is in danger."

"That's one of the things that's bothering me, Bill. Why is he still alive? I mean, if what I think happened actually did happen—"

"Oh, there's all sorts of possible reasons for that one, Frank. Most people don't know what killing their fellow man is all about, and when they do it for the first time it usually leaves a bad taste. It's very likely that they saw what they did to that poor Gonzalez fella and lost their motivation right there.

"But then again, these guys sound like professionals, so that's probably out. You said he left the country the next morning? Well, they missed their chance then, and after that the merger was announced, the deal was signed or whatever they do in one of these things, and there was probably no point in trying again."

I nodded, having considered these ideas already, but thinking it still didn't quite ring true.

"Bill, if they were excited enough to commit a murder, and if they were so meticulous in their planning, why did they leave it so late? He left the next day. This was their only shot."

"That's a good point. You said this CFO, what was his name?"

"Hurst. Sanford Hurst."

"Hurst said Spector sprung this on them. Well, maybe whoever did this really didn't have a lot of time to get it together. They planned a pretty good phony accident and hoped it would work. And when it didn't, they decided they missed the boat and let it go."

"Or maybe they're just waiting for another chance."

He smiled, pointing a fresh cigarette at me.

"You said it. And even if that's not the case, that's how we're gonna play it when we meet with Mr. Spector."

"We're going to meet him?"

"You bet. Leave that end to me, I know exactly how to talk to the executive assistant, secretary, or Boy Friday that this kinda guy always has around him. But you're coming along, especially since we're also going to drop by and see Mr. Robert Barstow."

"Bob Barstow?" I had told him about Barstow's involvement in the original insurance case and how he had dredged up the dirt on Gonzalez's alleged gambling. "What do we want with him?"

"Call it a professional courtesy if you like. Mr. Barstow is the one who set that tail on you."

Which made sense once I turned it over a few times in my head. Barstow had been sitting right there in Harvey's trailer when the insurance man had given me the address of Escobar's law firm. I'd been so pleased with tricking Harv into admitting his contact with Escobar that I'd overlooked the obvious connection. Those two guys in the tan sedan had picked me up in Davis because Barstow had tipped them off. There was a slight chance that Harv himself had placed that call, but it really wasn't his style, and I doubted very much that people like that would work with someone as dumb as Harv.

Before you get the wrong idea here, Haskell was not suggesting that we go and visit violence or even threats on Barstow. Private investigation work can sometimes come very close to breaking the law, but Bill had always warned me against it.

"First it's wrong, second it's too easy to get caught or ratted out, and third it's counterproductive. You pick up some evidence illegally and the next thing you know your whole case hinges on it. But it's not admissible in court, or you're sure you're going to get questioned about how you got it, and so your nice case goes right down the drain." I considered it funny to hear Bill Haskell talking about right and wrong, but I assumed he had rejiggered his priority list to fit his audience.

At any rate, we didn't have to go see Bob Barstow because Haskell had given it some thought during the night and decided against talking to him at all. He had given me a spot on his sofa and had announced his change of heart when he shook me awake that morning. He explained himself as we raced down the highway in his Mustang convertible.

"See, the problem with a guy like Bob is he's not half as smart as he thinks he is. So while I'm sure he thinks he knows who asked him to be on the lookout for you, he probably doesn't. We could explain to him that he's basically become an accessory to a murder—which he has—but then we'd really be tipping our hand and getting nothing in return. He'd give us some nonsense about a phantom beeper number or some other lie, and then sure as shootin' he'd be on the phone to those guys.

"And that wouldn't go along with what I've got in mind for Mr. Spector." His eyes took on that gleam again, and I decided he was much more interested in getting close to the former Hayward Shipping CEO than in solving my personal problems. He was dressed in a lightweight gray business suit with a pink tie, looking very much the socialite, and we were headed toward Spector's waterfront place in Davis at top speed.

As for me, I had been wearing the same set of clothes that morning that I'd been wearing for five days up until Haskell got a look at me. We had been headed to his office in Tallahassee so he could call Spector's secretary, and once we were there the Haskell machinery had kicked into high gear to make me look presentable.

In case you haven't already guessed, Bill Haskell was quite wealthy, all of it from many years accepting every case and never betraying a confidence, and his operation reflected his success. In addition to the five investigators on his payroll he had a top-notch office manager who demanded my jacket and trousers the instant I walked in the door. She didn't even look away as I stripped down to T-shirt and boxers. Instead she collected my things (including my tie) and disappeared around the corner to a one-hour dry cleaner's.

So even though I didn't look like the yacht club set, I was respectable enough in my newly cleaned and pressed clothes to pass for Haskell's assistant. Which was fine with me, as I didn't have the foggiest idea how to tell a multimillionaire that someone had probably tried to kill him two weeks before.

And without so much as a shred of evidence, I wasn't sure how Haskell was going to do that either.

F. Scott Fitzgerald is supposed to have once observed to Ernest Hemingway that "the rich are different from you and me." Hemingway allegedly replied, "Yes, they have more money." Or something very much like that. I know that quoting Hemingway is more of a Keys thing than a Panhandle thing, but the point here is that Drew Spector was different from me but not alien to my experience. He immediately reminded me of the moneyed people who had called me names while ruining my business.

That was not the case with Haskell, though. He and Spector were cut from the same cloth. I'd been hiding my underwear-clad form in a side office when Haskell made his phone calls to get on Spector's schedule. I wouldn't have given him any chance to get an appointment in less than a week, but he'd hit the right buttons and continued to bang on them as soon as we rolled up to the gate.

Spector's place wasn't all that big, but it was flanked by two other Davis money houses and a tall wrought-iron fence that ran along three sides of the property. The fourth side was the beach, and even though there was no way to block that off, it didn't look like too many clam diggers wandered across that stretch of coastline. We were met at the gate by some ex-NFL lineman, and even though he was friendly enough, it was clear he was part of the permanent security detail. Other men of similar dimensions were in evidence on the property, walking near the five-car garage or the pool or the beach, and I had to wonder how Spector ever got out on the public running path by himself.

The gate guy walked us straight through the front door of the two-story house. Spector made up for the house's relative smallness by packing it with expensive stuff, particularly in the front foyer. The floor was marble, the furniture was mahogany, and the vases were too valuable for anything but a padded box. I am no judge of art, but the seascapes and landscapes in the front hallway looked genuine to me.

We passed through a comfortable living room with a snow-white carpet and went straight out back across a raised deck that could have held fifty people. The big man was down on the sand, dressed all in white, and I put my sunglasses back on as we approached.

Haskell and Spector acted as if they were old fraternity brothers, with Haskell sticking his hand out stiff-arm while Spector was still five feet away. On closer inspection Spector was wearing light cotton pants, white sneakers, and a cream-colored V-neck sweater with a woven Harvard symbol on the chest. A collared shirt stuck out of the sweater, and he wore a set of black plastic sunglasses that would have made him look like a youthful John Kennedy if his hair had been just a bit lighter.

He didn't recoil from Haskell's assault, instead stepping in with a ready smile and grasping the outthrust hand in an almost tribal recognition. He asked if the drive down had been pleasant, completely ignoring me, and I hung back looking like the assistant I was supposed to be. I half expected to be asked to take a walk somewhere else by myself, but Haskell rescued me.

"This is Frank Cole, one of my guys." I let that pass, knowing it was a simple way of saying I was his gofer. "Frank is actually the guy who came across this."

Spector now regarded me with interest, if only for a moment, before extending his hand.

"In that case I believe I owe you my thanks."

"You're welcome, sir," I replied, playing the lackey to the hilt. I was still a bit surprised that he had believed our story, and I also wondered why he was at home when there were big goings-on at Hayward Shipping. I didn't have to wait long for the answer on that one.

"As I said on the phone, we have reason to believe you were the intended victim of an arranged hit-and-run homicide. May I show you some pictures?" Bill went right into his presentation, and I whipped open the folio I was carrying so that he could extract a picture of Eddie Gonzalez while he was alive.

"As you can see, Mr. Gonzalez would not have been mistaken for you in broad daylight, but the vehicle used to kill him had heavily tinted glass and the event occurred at sunset. He was wearing an orange reflector vest similar to the one you were wearing when Frank here saw you on the surveillance video of one of the properties bordering the fitness trail." The words simply rolled off his tongue.

"Any chance this is just a coincidence? Two men of similar build wearing reflector vests on the same jogging path isn't that hard to imagine."

"That's what we thought at first." I worked hard at keeping a straight face when I heard Bill use the plural pronoun, as I had been alone on this up until the previous night. "But the reason Frank was digging into this so hard was the lack of any motive for killing Mr. Gonzalez. In the meantime, the story of joyriding teenagers doesn't fit the locale, as the road in question is a winding residential boulevard that turns into the main business district. Although the local police believe this was a simple hit-and-run fatality, even Chief Tate in Bending Palms felt it was a bit out of place for that neighborhood."

Haskell was playing this well, stopping every few sentences to let Spector catch up or interject something. People who have reached Spector's status in life expect this kind of treatment.

"You know, Mr. Haskell, I'd still consider this an unlucky coincidence if it weren't for the local reaction to the merger." He made a gesture encompassing his house. "As you can see, I've had to lay on quite a bit of extra security since my return. I've received death threats."

"Yes, sir." Haskell nodded as he spoke, encouraging the other man to continue.

"But then again, all that has been since the announcement, nothing before it. And as upset as some of these people obviously are, I can't believe they'd go to these lengths just out of spite."

"It might not have been spite at all, sir. You mentioned the timing, and your instincts are dead-on. Whoever did this was trying to keep you from closing the impending deal."

"But my death wouldn't have done that. The board had already voted."

"According to the newspapers, Mr. Spector, the vote on this was a close one. With the sudden death of the CEO, a postponement might not have been out of the question."

Spector chewed on that one for a moment, thrusting his hands in his pockets and walking a few steps with his head down toward the sand. He turned after a moment.

"You know what you're saying?"

"I'm not accusing anyone, if that's what you mean, but logically this fits."

"My own board."

"Not necessarily the board, sir. Maybe someone who knew about the deal and thought there was a fair chance it would be postponed and eventually dumped if its primary architect were no longer in the picture."

It was clear that the wheels were grinding away in Spector's mind, and I began to wonder if he was as smart as the business papers said he was. He wasn't having a hard time accepting the story, but the reasoning behind it was escaping him. Perhaps our turnaround king was a specialist in saving disorganized companies because he didn't have the stuff to make a healthy one go.

"Let's walk a little," he said to Bill. I took it as my cue to head over to the deck. Clearly Spector wanted to discuss some sensitive arrangements with Haskell, and although I'd been accepted up until then, I was, after all, only the guy who had discovered the plot. One of the linebackers on the deck surprised me by offering to get me a coffee, and having nothing better to do I went with him into the kitchen.

The Spector kitchen was loaded with all of the most modern appliances, a range that could have fed an army, and a ton of chrome. One of those thirty-cup coffeepots was sitting up on a black countertop off to one side, obviously meant for the security detail's use, but the guard escorting me went to a low cupboard and found me a Styrofoam cup with a plastic lid. That didn't strike me as the action of an extra security man laid on recently, and so I guessed he was someone who normally guarded the Spector family.

"Kitchen's pretty clean for a household with kids," I said carefully, stirring in some sugar.

"Mrs. Spector and the children have gone back to New York," he replied softly, in a voice that sounded both concerned and regretful. "But I always had the impression we were just marking time down here anyway."

"How so?"

"I really shouldn't have said anything. Sorry, but I don't discuss the family with outsiders."

I thanked him for the coffee, and he escorted me back out onto the deck. We were just in time, as Haskell and Spector were shaking hands out on the sand. Business completed, Haskell headed toward me with purposeful strides. He glanced down at the coffee, gave me a quizzical look as if to ask "Making friends, are we?" and then we were back in the car and headed off down the road.

"Okay, he hired us." Bill had put the top up so we could talk. The car was eating the miles, but I could see we were headed back to Exile. "I told him it would be wise to get out of these parts until we figured out what was going on."

"His wife and kids are already gone."

"Very good, Frank. Always investigating. Yeah, he told me that, and it sounded like he meant to leave anyway. And I wouldn't be a bit surprised to see that house on the market soon."

"It seemed a little small."

"How do you mean?"

"He's a turnaround king, he comes in with big fanfare and even gets to put his own people on the board, but he buys a nice, efficient little place like that. He wanted a house where he'd be comfortable, but something he wouldn't have any trouble unloading in the year or so it would take to sell the company."

"You mean he had that in mind the whole time?"

"I do. That trick with the board proves it, and it was one of the first things he did. The Hayward board was loaded with insiders, and the stockholders had been on them for some time to put in some new blood. So Spector recommended some of his friends and then started working on the swing vote he'd need. He had this in mind when he took the job."

"Why?" For all of his worldliness, this was an area that Bill did not fully understand.

"Bill, ever notice there are sports coaches who are known for taking a flagging program and then getting it back on its feet? Well, you'll also see those same coaches moving around a lot. For some of them it's almost a contract job. They fix what's wrong and then hand it off so they can move on to the next challenge. But for a lot of them it's because they can't keep a good program running for a long time.

"Look at Spector's track record. Every company he ran was in the toilet. It's easy to come in and do tough things like sell departments and lay people off when the whole shebang is in jeopardy, but it gets much harder to do that when an outfit isn't doing badly. You have to manage costs while fighting a union that won't negotiate because nothing's wrong. You have to buy new equipment meant to boost productivity three years from now, but for those three years it's going to be a real drag on the bottom line.

"Spector's not one of those guys, and he was hired by an organization that wasn't in real trouble. So his best answer was to find a buyer, make a killing, and get outta Dodge."

Bill turned this over in his head, nodding. For once he looked impressed with me.

"When this is over, Frank, you're going to have to come up with a better reason for not coming on board with my firm."

"Don't start. I got into this case while doing a fool's errand for Harvey Webster. Next thing I know, someone puts a bullet on my kitchen table, a legitimate insurance claim is denied with my name on the reason, and a couple of thugs are tailing me.

"Speaking of which, does it make sense that if we identify those guys we come a lot closer to figuring this thing out?"

"Absolutely. That's why I'm going to move two of my guys into your place."

"I'm not going to play sitting duck for you." The meeting with Spector had really gotten my bile flowing. The image of the self-satisfied fat cat, no matter how concerned he was about his safety, had brought back unpleasant memories.

"You won't have to. I'm going to do a little digging of my own with some people I know, but in the meantime you're going to be doing what you do best. I need complete backgrounds on the entire Hayward board, including the new guys, as well as their relatives.

"I've got all of the licensing and access from my office, so all you have to do is find and compile it. I'll be visiting the board people personally, but I need the background stuff first."

"You sure it's someone on the board?"

"Not at all. Murders are funny things, Frank, in that they're usually committed by irrational people. Right now we believe that the people who did this were in a position to change Spector's decision in the event of his death. That's a good assumption, even though that particular net spreads way beyond the board.

"But our real problem is if this was just some Hayward Shipping stevedore with a brother in organized crime. Some dockworker who thinks he's gonna lose his job." He stopped for a moment, as if taken aback by his own words. He brightened immediately after that, though. "But, hey, it'll be fun to hang around with the Davis money set for a while even if that is the case."

CHAPTER SIX

So that was how I went from living in my car to using all the gee-whiz Internet gadgetry in Bill Haskell's office. Although it was much nicer to have access to Haskell's apartment, and it was surely better to be safely tucked away in Tallahassee than walking the streets of Exile, let me just say that Paula Walsh, Haskell's office manager, was no Mary Beth Marquadt. Whereas the Exile reference librarian would do anything to help anyone, Paula seemed to view me as some kind of invader and clearly couldn't wait for me to leave.

I would have thought that Haskell's boyish excitement over landing a fish like Spector would have naturally passed on to the woman who handled the office finances, but perhaps that was asking a bit much. Bill ensconced me in his own office, giving the excuse that I needed a quiet place to work and that he almost never used the room, but that further elevation of my status did not put me in a better light with Paula.

She had been vaguely disapproving of me when I handed her my wrinkled suit that morning, but by the time Haskell headed out the door that afternoon I wondered which one of us would be alive when he returned. She raced through the access procedures for the various pay-to-use databases to which Haskell Investigations subscribed, barely giving me enough time to get it all down on paper. She then explained, rather forcefully, that there were several nice places to eat within easy walking distance, clearly concerned that I might be crazy enough to ask her to order me lunch. Frankly, she intimidated me so completely that I didn't poke my head out until late in the afternoon.

Haskell had headed off to redirect some of his people to the case, and I knew he wanted the background information right away, but I took a few minutes to walk around his office anyway. The carpet was a mustard gold, same as in the entrance hallway, and the walls were paneled in imitation wood. Much of his floor space was taken up by a sofa, a circular coffee table, and two armchairs, which made we think that this particular room was used mainly for landing clients. The walls were festooned with various licenses (Haskell had gone to the trouble of getting licensed as a PI in most of the neighboring states), pictures of Haskell receiving awards, and a large metal key on a plaque which turned out to be the key to the city of Tallahassee.

Having procrastinated long enough, I hung my jacket on the back of Bill's high-backed desk chair and set to work. The PC keyboard looked brand-new, the chair was absolutely the wrong piece of furniture for prolonged typing, and I made a mental note that Bill Haskell probably used the machine for e-mail only, if that.

Hours later, having gone into some marvelous fee-based data systems, I came away with the basic information on Hayward Shipping's board of directors and even some of their relatives. Identifying who was on the board was easy, as the company was incorporated in Florida and so the data was readily at hand through the state government sites as well as their annual report. Going from there, it was a snap to determine whether any of them had ever done time (they hadn't) or broken the law (they had, but it was all small stuff, like mouthing off to the wrong policeman).

This kind of data mining feeds on itself, and so I frequently switched back and forth between the data providers' sites and the basic news services as an item from one source suggested more detailed information in another. The board members' business biographies had been available in Hayward Shipping's literature, but expanded versions were frequently available from alumni sites and charitable organizations. These men were prominent figures in the local business community, and news articles covering various civic-award presentations often revealed basic information that the business biographies did not.

When I say men, I mean men, as there were no women on the Hayward board. For many years the men who ran Hayward had been a collegial gang of four who approved whatever the CEO wanted. It was probably inaccurate to refer to the head guy at Hayward as a CEO prior to Spector's arrival, for he was most commonly referred to as the president of the board in older company literature. The current CFO, Sanford Hurst, was the kingmaker who had found Spector for them and had been the president of the board for two decades before stepping down.

Spector had come in at the right time, as Hayward had been under considerable pressure to modernize its management practices. Shareholders had become increasingly vocal over the years about the chummy club that was the board room, criticizing it for having so few outsiders and being so small. Spector had responded to this by expanding the governing body from four to seven and bringing in three outsiders he had met earlier in his career. He had even brought a woman along, and by expanding the board to an odd number of seats had dropped the CEO's vote from their proceedings. The previous CEO had held the deciding vote in the event of a tie, but everything about the old company suggested that votes were never that close—if they had been taken at all.

These issues seem straightforward, but they are not. Having outsiders on a board is supposed to broaden the experience level and avoid groupthink, and it often does. However, it also runs the risk of bringing in professional board members, people who hold directors' chairs with numerous companies and have difficulty getting to all those pesky meetings. In the meantime, some industries are so complex that it is probably a good idea to draw the people making the big decisions from industry veterans or even people who have been with the company for decades.

I guess I'm trying to say that this is not a one-size-fits-all magic bullet, but that it plays well with the corporate governance crowd and that Spector might have been blindly applying a widely accepted nostrum. His later decision to sell the company, and the considerable effort it must have taken to flip one of the old-style Hayward directors, suggested that he had been planning to hijack the board all along, but I now began to question that. Even if he had come to Florida intending to sell a perfectly healthy shipping company, it did not sound logical that the previous board would have let him expand the governing body in such a way that he could easily do that. There was very little background information on that particular development, however, and I had to keep moving.

After assembling the basic personal stuff, I got into Hayward's finances. Now, even an accountant will shy away from trying to interpret the financial statements of a business from outside, just because there is so much pertinent data that never makes it onto those pages, but after reviewing their filings for five years I couldn't for the life of me see why they'd brought in a turnaround expert. It simply hadn't been necessary. Their revenues were solid, their debt was manageable, and their loss record was marginal when you remembered they ran shipping throughout the Caribbean. Selling the place had clearly stirred up a hurricane of protest all over the Gulf Coast, and I could easily imagine a few unhappy campers among the old Hayward directors, watching the whiz kid sell a company that was doing fine on its own.

What I couldn't determine was just who had gone over to the other side. The vote had been four to three, and under Hayward's new rules that had been enough to authorize Spector's sale of the company. Of course, it had to be approved by the stockholders, but their share values had taken a nice jump when the news had been released and they were not likely to vote against something that put more money in their pockets. Sanford Hurst had been screaming Spector's name from most of the rooftops in Davis, but he had somehow neglected to divulge who among his old cronies had switched sides and voted with Spector's three acolytes. Regardless of how secret the balloting had been, inside the group they always knew who did what. And regardless of corporate secrecy, that kind of information always gets out. This time they didn't seem to know or they weren't saying. It didn't fit.

In the meantime I did come across something that was going to require further investigation. Sanford Hurst's son and namesake was apparently quite the problem child. He had been arrested for what looked like grand theft auto about a year before, and even though he had been a minor at the time it had made it into court as a much lesser offense. His father's influence probably helped him, as the case was dismissed, but there were ominous references to previous brushes with the law. Apparently Sanford junior liked to drive fast and punch people, and just seeing that in print about such a wealthy family said that his hidden career in these pursuits was extensive.

The part that really caught my eye came after that, in a recent society column where Sanford junior was lauded for discovering a thirst for knowledge abroad. He'd been selected by a prestigious foundation for a program of study in Europe even though the selection process for that particular award had closed months before. The story explained that Sanford junior had missed a slot on the original slate by a hair, but that one of the winners had canceled unexpectedly. All of this had happened since the accident.

This is where the search of the standard databases comes up short. By focusing on criminal records and court filings, guys like me frequently miss big news like this. I had been moving back and forth between the pay-to-use services and the basic Internet searches, and by using the information from one to search the other I had come across this nugget. It might be nothing, but I was definitely going to mention it to Haskell.

If this process sounds boring, it is. In addition to the monotony, I was virtually a prisoner in that office and began wondering if that was what Bill had had in mind by dropping me there. He now owned the case and the client, his men were sitting in my house in Exile hoping my trackers returned, and at this point I could only foul things up if I went back there. I had never really explained my lack of interest in making money at this new job, so it was even possible that Haskell feared having to share whatever fee he had negotiated with Spector.

I typed up some brief notes about what I had gotten from the Web, making it all nice and neat for whenever Haskell came back. Most of a report like that is simply a printout from the Internet, and I had gotten a volley of abuse from Paula when I had run all that off on the printer in the hall. Some people are territorial like that, and I decided to help her out by getting lost.

While considering Haskell's motivation for leaving me in his office, it had also occurred to me that I had removed from the game the only individual looking into the death of Eddie Gonzalez. It might sound ancillary at this point, but everything we knew had come from the investigation of Eddie's demise. Additionally, I was probably in much less danger now that we had lined up the CEO of Hayward Shipping. Spector had agreed to speak with his corporate counsel about arranging interviews with the board, so the cat was definitely out of the bag regarding Haskell's involvement. Whoever had left that bullet for me was either going to have to kill an awful lot of people or leave me alone. So there was no reason to stay in hiding any longer.

In the meantime, there were still loose ends with Eddie Gonzalez's insurance, and I wanted to be able to hand Mike Escobar some pretty solid investigative stuff about Eddie's gambling experience. A few rumors could get a claim flagged if the insurers wanted to see things that way, but putting some written testimony in the hands of a paralegal with lawyer friends might make them see it differently.

I was already quite familiar with Farragut Community College because I was currently a photography student there. When I had started doing background work, Haskell had suggested I get familiar with basic photography because so much of investigative work involves cameras of one kind or another. I have learned since then that a good video camera can do most of the work I would have handled, things like witness statements and insurance footage, but there were other benefits to taking the course at Farragut.

I didn't really notice the biggest benefit when I first started taking the course, largely because I was still wandering about in a postbankruptcy daze. Her name was Beth Ann Thibedault, she was bright and pretty, and she taught the course. Although we were not dating officially, we usually went for coffee after class ended and I learned that I had impressed her by being the only man in the class who had not asked her out.

Personally I suspect that Beth Ann had a houseful of stray cats and that I aroused her maternal instinct, but for the first few months I was in Florida I was definitely one of the walking wounded, and I am sure she picked up on that. It bothered me that I had missed class for the first time a few nights before, but the memory of the bullet telegram put that in perspective. Even so, I felt it was time for a trip to the college.

I had packed some casual clothes when I fled my place, and so I changed to look more like a student when I rolled up to the big parking lot outside the student union that evening. Farragut didn't have much in the way of dorms, but the student union was always well attended, even at night. There was no chance that I would pass for an undergrad, but I had no intention of trying some half-baked undercover routine anyway, and instead walked up to the first campus cop I saw.

If it had been earlier in the day I would have located one of Farragut's accounting classrooms and tried to strike up a conversation with Eddie's former classmates, but that wouldn't fly now. This late there was very little likelihood that I would identify the budding accountants among the kids drinking beer, eating burgers, and trying to study. A campus cop would either blow me off or help me out, and there was very little I could do if it was the former. I decided to try the honest approach, figuring a cop is a cop and that he would see right through one of my little white lies.

This one looked like he might help out. If he had been one of those lean, fit types with the prison guard buzz cut and active eyes I wouldn't have even bothered, but he was older, alert but not obtrusive, and a fair-sized gut stuck out over his utility belt. As a bonus he looked bored, so I walked right up and shook his hand.

"Hi, Officer, I'm Frank Cole with Haskell Investigative Services, you may have heard of us." I didn't think there was anything wrong with throwing Bill's name around, seeing as he'd given me free run of his office that very afternoon.

"Hi there. Yeah, I've heard of Haskell before." He smiled evenly, and I scratched him off the list of security guards who secretly want to be private eyes.

“I’m up here looking into the death of a former student, a young man named Eddie Gonzalez.” I proffered a photo, but he didn’t let me get any farther.

“You and half of Florida. Who was that kid, anyway? With all the folks tracking him, you’d think he was the quarterback for the ’Noles.”

“Well, I had heard there was another PI through here a few days ago, a guy named Bob Barstow.”

“Yep. I didn’t talk to him, but I sure heard about him. Listen, Mr. Cole, I’m not going to be able to help you much. We got a briefing just a day ago saying the college was about to get sued because somebody said we have a gambling ring up here and that this kid was somehow involved. They told us to refer any new questions to public relations.”

He said it in a dismissive way, as if he had a low opinion of whoever had given that directive, and I decided to see where that went.

“You get that a lot?”

“Yep. Too much, considering we’ve been warning them about this for a long time. Heck, this thing is so big now that we’ve got all sorts of people, not even students, all over campus taking down bets. If they’d listened to us at the beginning we could have cleaned this up.”

“You sound like you know who some of the players are.”

“That I do, but honestly I can’t keep talking to you like this. For all I know you’re with that law firm, the one causing all the trouble.”

“Tanner and Briscoe? Out of Davis?”

“That’s them.” Apparently Mike Escobar had not been exaggerating when he mentioned the legal heat he could muster.

“What if I told you I am definitely not with them, and that I’m trying to show that what happened to Eddie Gonzalez was not linked to gambling?”

He shook his head. “Been lied to before. No offense, but I’m not going to get fired for being stupid.”

"Got it. I understand, really. One last thing, you can answer it or not, it's up to you. You think that whatever's going on up here is heavy enough that somebody might actually get killed for it?"

He looked around him for a moment before answering.

"Like I said, there are a lot of new faces around here because of this gambling business. Who can say how heavy these guys are? Me, I never understood how anyone can collect from a dead man, but people get killed over money all the time."

Boy, that was not what I wanted to hear.

Someone had thoughtfully let the air out of one of my tires while I was inside. I looked at the black omega that used to be my front driver's-side tire and then looked around to see if some giggling frat boys were watching. I should have been smarter than that, as the leering face of Bob Barstow approached nonchalantly. He was every bit as seedy as he looked when I last saw him at Harvey Webster's trailer.

"Looks like you got yourself a flat, Frank," he announced in a loud voice. His hands were in the side pockets of a set of brown pants that matched the light jacket slung over his shoulder. It was hot outside, and his hat was tipped back on his head. "Probably somebody who didn't appreciate you propping a nail against their tire where they'd be sure to run over it."

"Campus security cameras are all over here, Bob," I lied, knowing that Farragut didn't have the budget for that. He didn't even blink.

"Maybe they'll help you find who did this. After all, you're not likely to figure anything out on your own, are you?"

"What brings you here, Bob?" I asked as I walked toward the trunk.

"A little education. You see, that Gonzalez kid was just the tip of the iceberg out here. They got a heck of a lot of people laying bets on this campus, and somebody hired me to look into it a little more." He grinned so that all his teeth showed. "You're the gift that keeps on giving, Frank. First you help me connect the dots with Sun Provident, and then you drop my name with Mike Escobar. He figured I was already a few laps down the track on this, so bang! A whole new job."

Someone had been in my trunk as well. My spare was gone.

"Ya know, most sneak thieves will dump a heavy item like that tire somewhere after they've lugged it for a while. If you look in the bushes, or in the Dumpsters, you might find it."

I turned and started toward him, not knowing what I was going to do because I haven't been in a fight since grade school. I got lucky, though, as a familiar voice called my name uncertainly.

"Frank? Is that you?"

I turned to see the slim figure of Beth Ann Thibedault approaching. In a moment I also saw that Bob Barstow was in far greater danger from her than from me.

"Mr. Barstow, if you're not off the grounds in one minute I am going to call security." She stormed across the parking lot from Farragut's administration building, dressed in a light sleeveless top and white shorts. She was only a part-time teacher here and this was not one of her class nights, but even in that getup she looked ready to tear Bob in half for his involvement in suing the school.

They must have butted heads before, because he smiled innocently and began backing away.

"I'm sorry, Miss Thibedault, I was just helping one of my colleagues from the investigation business. He seems to have a flat. Maybe you could get one of your rent-a-cops to change it for him."

He vanished in the darkness, and I got the full wrath of someone I was thinking of asking out on a date.

"And just what are you doing here talking to . . . that?" She was clearly horrified that I might be assisting Barstow with the lawsuit investigation.

“Beth Ann, he’s the one who gave me the flat tire.” I motioned to the empty inside of my trunk. “And then stole my spare. I am not working with him.”

“He did this? I *am* calling security.” She started marching straight for the student union, but I caught her arm with just the tips of my fingers as she passed.

“Forget it. He didn’t slash my tire, just let the air out. And if I walk around long enough I’ll find the spare.” I decided not to tell her that this was payback for my trick with the common nail, or that I now knew that it had been a childish and dangerous thing to do. I could only imagine what Barstow would have done if my act of vandalism had involved his car instead of Harvey’s. I took a flashlight out of the trunk and shut the hatch with a thud.

Beth Ann spoke with the voice of frustration.

“He’s been all over here, asking all sorts of questions about student gambling, apparently for some Davis law firm that’s going to sue the college. Like this place is made of money.” She bit her lower lip for a moment and then relaxed completely, as if she’d put the whole thing out of her mind. I’d only seen her do that once before, but I really wanted to learn how she accomplished that trick. She turned to me and said, “So you think he ditched your spare right around here?”

I slept on Beth Ann’s couch that night. As I said, we’re not even dating, but she knows what I do and that I am not made of money and so she didn’t object when I asked for a little floor space. I hadn’t told her about losing my business yet, but that would also entail telling her about losing my wife in the bargain and I’m just not up to that right now. Besides, since we’re still only coffee buddies, it’s not as if I’m hiding anything.

Yes, I’m divorced, and that hurts a lot. You could say I married money, but I was pretty well off myself when Lisa and I got hitched and so that was not the reason. And her wealthy background played a role in splitting us up when my company went belly-up, so it's not as if I got anything out of her family's fortune. They'd been horrified when my business began taking on water, and the very notion of someone in their family going bankrupt had been too much for them and the country club set. Not that any of them had ever had to work for a living or had the basic sense to pour sand out of a boot, but you can see where my animosity toward Spector came from.

The sad truth was I still miss her and keep telling myself that she'd divorced me for her family's sake and that she would have stuck with me if they hadn't been causing so much trouble. Yes, I know, that doesn't make any sense at all, but it doesn't change the fact that every time the phone rings late at night I am convinced it's going to be Lisa.

That might be another reason why I haven't gone past the coffee stage with Beth Ann, although sleeping on her couch was a quantum leap in the glacial pace of our relationship. I took it as a good sign that she was still in a T-shirt and running shorts, her sleeping attire, when she woke me the next morning. It was a gesture of some intimacy, and when she announced she was making breakfast I decided I was definitely going to formally ask her out.

When the case was over, anyway.

"So what are you working on that's got you up here overnight?" she asked brightly as I padded into the kitchen. The smell of coffee and bacon met me, and she handed me an empty cup when I began looking around.

"It's about an accounting student here, Eddie Gonzalez, he's from the town I live in and he got run over almost three weeks ago."

I watched her moving the bacon around. My best estimate placed her at twenty-five, with lean runner's legs and no fat at all. She had a girl-next-door face with brown eyes and dark hair that curved from the top of her head to her shoulders, and more than one unsuspecting student had mistaken her for a pushover in class. That sweet demeanor vanished once she stood up in front of a group of students, and if you showed up unprepared she made you pay for it. And this was in a weekly photography class she taught at night, so I can only imagine what she did to customers at her day job at the camera store.

"Yeah, I heard about that. Awful. So what have they got you looking at?"

I wasn't sure how much of the story to tell her, for a variety of reasons. Obviously I didn't want to scare her with the bullet story, but after the campus cop's observations the night before I was also concerned that she might consider me a paranoid. Up until then I had been operating on the assumption that Eddie didn't have an enemy in the world, but according to the security guy that might not be the case. So if Eddie had run afoul of the wrong people, my bullet-dropping visitors might have actually gotten the guy they were after and been unhappy that I was looking into it. This would not only make Bob Barstow and Harv right about the insurance claim's illegitimacy, but it would make me look like an idiot to Beth Ann.

"Well, at first it looked like a simple accident and the insurance people were suspicious because Eddie had bought a policy just a few weeks before. So I was doing the background work when Barstow heard a rumor that Eddie was involved in some gambling up here. I had already discovered that Eddie was getting ready to get married, and that was why he'd bought the insurance, but it turns out they were looking for any excuse to flag the claim, and so they decided the gambling was criminal activity."

"So that's why the school is getting sued."

"That story does seem to be getting around. You see, I talked to one of Eddie's high school buddies, and he told me Eddie wasn't heavy into gambling." I decided that Anneliese Escobar's pregnancy was definitely out of bounds, but there was no way to tell the story without mentioning her. "That buddy is the same guy behind the lawsuit. He works at a law firm. Eddie was going to marry his sister, and now there's a chance Eddie might have been more deeply involved than I was told. And I'm not sure what to do at this point. I mean, how do you prove a negative?"

"You might not need to. Did you say the guy bringing the suit knew about the gambling?"

"Yeah, but he didn't think Eddie was that heavily involved."

"And he's just a paralegal in that firm?"

"Right." She was smiling at me, and I got the strange feeling I had missed something.

"Well, I doubt very much that he'd risk getting fired if he knew this buddy of his was gambling a lot. It's one thing to get a lawyer friend to look at a suit, but it's quite another to do it with people in your own office." The simplicity of her comment was pure genius, and it lifted the weight of the security guard's opinion off my shoulders in a rush. She dropped a plate of bacon and eggs in front of me and I thought I was in heaven.

She joined me at the table, still smiling, and it came out.

"I'm divorced."

"I figured."

"I like you."

"I like you."

"Look, when I get this case finished—"

"Eat."

"Tanner and Briscoe law offices, Michael Escobar speaking. May I help you?"

"Hello, Michael. This is Frank Cole."

"Mr. Cole!" That same mocking tone was back. "Thought you'd gone back up north."

"In a way I did. I've been up at Farragut trying to clear Eddie's name."

"How's that comin' along?" More mockery.

"Pretty good, if I wanted the insurance claim to get denied. The place is locked up tighter than a drum. It seems somebody is suing the school."

"Imagine that."

"Look, Escobar, I'd just as soon drop this thing and go fishing, know what I mean? But I have a question. If Eddie wasn't really deep in the betting up at Farragut, how come everybody thinks he was? I talked to a local cop near there"—I didn't want to burn the campus cop who'd helped me—"and as far as he's concerned this place is Las Vegas. So if Eddie owed money to the wrong people, there are quite a few folks who are ready to believe they'd kill him over it."

A short silence over the phone. Escobar began speaking more softly, and I got an image in my head of the young man bent double in his seat with his head under his desk.

"Listen, it's not a lawsuit; it's the threat of a lawsuit. And now Farragut's lawyers are calling Sun Provident's lawyers making the same threats. After all, Sun Provident got them into this."

An eye for an eye until the whole world goes blind. The next time I see my old buddy Mark I'm going to punch him just for becoming a lawyer.

"And what if Sun Provident coughs up my cop buddy or somebody like him, somebody who's going to refer to the college as Farragut Community Casino?"

"You're on a different time line than the legal profession, Mr. Cole." I'd heard that one before. People who are losing an argument frequently make reference to secret information that you don't have. "There's a sweating period—"

"Who do you think you're talking to? Remember that bankruptcy you looked up? The one with my name on it? They sweated me for three years, and in the end all they got was the company name. And with the way you clowns are going, Sun Provident's gonna make the case that Eddie was waist deep in something that got him killed.

"Just out of idle curiosity, do you have anyone besides yourself who can testify that Eddie wasn't beyond the nickel-and-dime betting?" Even if they did, no one was watching Eddie all day every day, so who knows what he was really up to?

"The best kind of witness there is, Mr. Cole. That's who we've got. Don't go worrying about our case." There was a voice behind him, and he hung up.

Beth Ann had already headed off to work, and even though she'd said it was okay for me to use her phone, I wasn't going to treat the place like Haskell's office. I'd been right about the stray cat thing, by the way, as she had three of them. One of them, a calico with long hair, hopped up on my lap while I sat at her desk and tried to figure out what Escobar had just told me.

What kind of witness would a paralegal consider best? An eyewitness maybe, but this wasn't a case of proving Eddie did something; in fact, it was the exact opposite. A corroborating witness, perhaps, but that would just place Eddie somewhere else at a certain moment in time, and once again it wouldn't prove he wasn't gambling heavily. Even if they could produce whatever passed for a bookmaker at Farragut and the guy testified that Eddie hadn't placed a bet in weeks, it wouldn't do much for them because Eddie could have just switched bookies.

Escobar himself was out as a possibility, working a demanding job and only seeing Eddie outside of Farragut. It was nice that he felt Eddie didn't do too much of this stuff, but he was also the beneficiary's brother and so not a candidate for the witness stand. The campus cop had referred to the gambling action as an ongoing thing, so it was unlikely that a mysterious federal task force had cleaned the place out a few months before. Don't laugh; Haskell could tell you about a case that collapsed when a witness testified to a meeting in a building that had been torn down a month before the sit-down was alleged to have taken place.

Besides, even if every bookie at the college had been hauled off to jail it wouldn't mean that Eddie hadn't branched out. If somebody wants to lay down a bet, they can do it a lot of different ways, and maybe that was something I had overlooked. A little friendly sports betting with the frat boys can get you in over your head fast, but it just doesn't fit the mold of getting run over for a debt. But if the frat boys introduced you to the wrong people it sure could. Maybe that was what the campus cop had been trying to tell me all along.

I came back to the expert witness question, and thinking of it that way was what answered it. Escobar hadn't called his witness an expert, but that was about all that was left. Someone with high levels of training in a certain field, someone who works in that field, someone who holds certifications showing expertise. A cop, maybe.

Or the police chief of Exile. The same guy who told me Eddie was squeaky clean.

"Hi, Chief. May I speak with you?" Dannon was in the outer office talking to Paul, one of two full-time officers on the Exile payroll. Dannon seemed to hire these guys for size, as both Pete and Paul were big, muscular men in their twenties. Peter and Paul. I had never noticed that before.

"Hello, Frank." He didn't seem any friendlier, but he ushered me into his office and shut the door.

"Want to tell me why Haskell is staking out your house?" He hadn't even sat down behind his desk yet.

"Sure. If you'll tell me why you lied about Eddie Gonzalez."

A statement like that is what I refer to as taking a big chance. Southern law enforcement is a different beast from what I was used to up north, and in a town the size of Exile no one talks to the chief of police that way. Especially not some Northern wannabe private eye making trouble for a local family.

"I didn't lie to you. I told you Eddie was a great guy and he was. I personally grabbed him by the shirtfront and warned him that if he didn't stop gambling I was going to break every bone in his body."

"So you knew all about this but didn't tell me."

"Let's understand each other, Frank. I'm the chief of police, not an insurance collector. You came to me trying to take the easy way out, trying to use our friendship to get dirt on a dead man, and I did what I do with any inquiry like that. I showed you the door."

"You told me he was spotless."

"Okay, I told you what I am prepared to say on the stand, and then I showed you the door. And I stand by what I said. He was a great kid, he worked like a dog, and I put the fear of God in him about this betting business." He shrugged. "Heck, he never had any money anyway. It was all five- and ten-dollar action."

It was not easy to know what to make of this. Up north the lawyers would have torn Dannon to pieces on the stand just asking how much time he spent with Eddie prior to the accident. But down here he had more than a little status, much of it based on watching Gonzalez grow up right in front of him. He was an expert witness in law enforcement, but he was also an expert witness in the town of Exile as well. In fact, they could probably toss Chief Tate up there and find out Dannon was pretty near an expert witness about Bending Palms, too.

My buddy Mark had once said that knowing your judge was half the battle, and down here I bet he would have extended that to knowing your audience. Up north, where television has colored the image of every cop who ever raises his right hand and swears to tell the truth, and where some parents don't see their own kids for days on end, the concept of a police officer testifying to a young man mending his ways is pretty laughable stuff. Down here it isn't. In Exile it isn't.

"Chief, all the way through this investigation I've banged my head up against whether or not Eddie was gambling enough to get murdered. There's basically no way to prove he'd quit, or to establish whether or not he was behind enough to get in trouble. And your keeping quiet didn't help."

"Frank, what was Eddie doing when he died?"

"Jogging. You know that."

"Yes I do. I'd seen him just a few nights before, and he didn't have a care in the world. He was pretty excited about getting married, but there wasn't anything bothering him. And not a mark on him."

He said the last part pointedly.

"You're saying that he would have gotten some warning before somebody actually killed him for a debt."

"That's the way they work it, Frank. Dead people don't pay off, and they get into the rough stuff gradually. I can tell you right now that no one was leaning on that kid."

Bill Haskell had called Chief Dannon before his people took up residence inside my house. According to Bill, it is prudent to inform the local police when you are conducting surveillance, particularly in a residential area where the locals are likely to notice a stranger hanging around. I really did not expect anyone sinister to be dropping by the house now that it had been empty for so long and so many new people were obviously investigating Eddie Gonzalez's accident, so I called the guys at the number Haskell had given the chief.

I didn't really know too many of Haskell's people and didn't recognize the voice on the cell phone. Even so, he liked the idea when I offered to come by and possibly scare up some game for them. I made the offer on the assumption that they had already decided that this was a dry hole and would be getting bored, but my real intention in visiting was to get a shower in my own home and retrieve my front-door key from my home's current occupants.

When I got there I parked out front and walked right through the front door. No one had followed me at any time since I had returned to Exile, and the street was almost empty. The place looked the same with the exception that someone had closed the blinds, and I was greeted at the door.

I had spoken to a rough male voice on the phone, but the investigator who confronted me was a woman. I had seen a picture of her on the wall of Haskell's office, surrounded by martial arts awards, and meeting her in person confirmed my initial belief that she could kick me across the room. She was almost my height, with sandy blond hair cut very close on the sides and not much longer on the top. She was wearing a light brown suit similar to mine, and it seemed clear that she had impersonated me when they got there.

"I'm Rhonda Walker." She shook my hand firmly while motioning behind her with a callused thumb. "And this is Teddy." A huge bald man with a black beard, wearing a black T-shirt and jeans, waved from my couch. I couldn't resist.

"As in Teddy Bear?"

"Heard of me, huh? Yeah, it's Baer, B-A-E-R, but Teddy's just a nickname." He didn't bother sharing his true first name, and since he seemed friendly I didn't push him. Rhonda spoke.

"How long have you lived here?" She sounded mildly annoyed at the place.

"Seven, eight months. Why?"

"It would have helped us if it looked like you actually lived here.

You see, once a normal person's lived in a place for a while they usually get the paper delivered, or let people know the new address so they get mail.

"And that way, when I hopped out of a cab this morning dressed like you, I would have scooped up all the old papers, emptied the mailbox, and basically let anyone driving by know that you had come back. They would have noticed that the mail and the papers had been collected. But the way you live, mister, you could go on vacation for a year and the place would look the same."

"That really threw off our act." This came from Teddy on the couch, easily picking up the thread when his partner stopped talking. "I started out this morning up the street watching the front door, but after an hour we saw that no one could tell Rhonda was even in here."

"She closed the blinds. They could tell from that."

Teddy shrugged and went back to the paper, so I crossed to the answering machine and played its only new message. I'd been pretty good about calling in and checking, but this one was two days old and I could only hope it wasn't something embarrassing. That got more humorous the more I thought about it. Here I was, having turned over my home to two strangers, worrying about what they'd think about a phone message that they'd probably already played. I looked at the kitchen table and saw that the bullet and the newspaper article were gone, presumably for some kind of fingerprint testing that would reveal nothing.

They had brought two large black canvas bags with straps and zippers that now sat on the living room floor, but only one was open. From what I could see it contained a camera tripod, some rolled electrical cable, and probably some video camera gear. It was probably a standard kit for this kind of work, but they hadn't bothered setting any of it up.

The phone message clicked on, and it was my buddy and lawyer, Mark Ruben. He sounded subdued.

"Hey, Frank, it's Mark. Nothing of an emergency nature here, but I finally heard from our friends and wanted to keep you in the loop. You were right on the money about this one. They're holding out for the patents and they don't think this thing's going anywhere in appellate court anytime soon. As I said before, there's talk of pending legislation and everybody's taking a hands-off approach at the moment.

"I'm gonna work that angle from here, but the status of the patents is turning into a real issue. There's no telling if we'll be able to cut the insurance people out of that side of things, even if we get an appeal date. Sorry this isn't any better news, buddy."

Mark was a fast talker, even for a lawyer, and he spat that out as if he'd rehearsed it. At moments like this I had a hard time connecting the voice on the phone to the guy who used to get drunk with me on Saturday nights in school. He finished up fast.

"Call me back when you get in. I saw Lisa in the society pages, looks great, I didn't know if you wanted to hear that but . . . well, call me back when you get in. Talk soon."

The last bit about my ex-wife showing up on the social scene bothered me more than the nonnews about my appeal. It must have shown, as Teddy smiled at me over the newspaper.

"That your lawyer?"

"Yes."

"It's always a bad sign when they start calling you 'buddy.' You need to fire him and get another one." He shook the paper straight and disappeared behind it.

CHAPTER SEVEN

Having Rhonda and Teddy in my house was probably what set me straight again. Rhonda moved around a lot, as if unable to suppress a rambunctious energy, while Teddy remained almost motionless on the sofa. Either way, they seemed convinced that this part of the trail was cold, and they were probably right.

I tried to think of what their boss was doing at that moment. According to our last conversation, Haskell was digging for dirt on the Hayward Shipping board of directors. He was doing this because they were the only people who could have reversed Spector's decision to sell the company and were, therefore, prime suspects.

On my side of things, I had been trying to confirm the good name of the deceased because I wanted his girlfriend to get the insurance money. Looking at the two sides of the operation in this fashion made both approaches look pretty foolish, as neither one was likely to tell us who actually hit Eddie Gonzalez with that SUV. Presumably the murderers were the same people who put the bullet in my house, so Rhonda and Ted were actually the only ones covering the place where the two investigations intersected.

Unfortunately, there was very little chance that the people who had wanted to scare me would be back at my house ever again. By contacting Spector we had let them know I was no longer working this case alone, so even Rhonda and Teddy were wasting their time. The key here was the same as it had been at the beginning: Find out who was driving that SUV when it hit Eddie Gonzalez. Digging up dirt on the board or verifying Eddie's character was not going to do that because they were two completely unrelated activities.

What we needed to do was investigate the intersection of the people who had left me the bullet and a dead man who was supposed to have been Drew Spector. Eddie was almost an ancillary part of the equation, as his death had almost certainly been accidental. So what was the intersection of the bad guys and Spector? This intersection was not a geographic location, as Finch Boulevard was simply one of many spots on that trail which could have been used for the deed. Nor was it a point in time, as Spector hadn't even gone jogging that night.

No. The intersection, the nexus, was the SUV. The killers had stolen it so they could use it as a murder weapon. They had selected it because it was heavy, it had a protected grille, and the windows were tinted. They had chosen it because it was close by and because it had not moved in weeks. They could have chosen an SUV normally parked on a neighboring street near Finch Boulevard, but there was always the chance that the vehicle's owner might decide to use it that night, ruining everything. They needed something they could count on, and they could count on the truck parked at Jason's Subaru.

How had the killers known that? They were a careful bunch, professional in every way, and they would have wanted to be sure about this crucial point. That meant surveillance. Someone would have been watching that SUV, or at least checking it to see if it had moved at all in the days prior to the accident.

These people were also planning for unfortunate developments, which was why they had wanted the tinted glass. Although the jogging trail was relatively deserted at that time of night, there was always a chance someone would see them racing away and so they had to have the tint. There was also a chance that someone would call the police and identify the speeding SUV, so they had to separate themselves from the vehicle right away. That was why they doubled back to the secluded parking spot farther up the trail.

This all added up to meticulous planning and an almost paranoid consideration of what could go wrong. Going back to the truck parked in the overflow lot of Jason's Subaru, there might even have been a chance that the SUV would not start at the moment they attempted to steal it. So what would they do about that? Although no one seemed to know what time the vehicle was stolen, the odds were good it was taken less than an hour before it was used as a murder weapon, maybe even less. To take it the night before would risk a report of its theft and bring the cover of irresponsible teen hooligans into question.

All of this suggested that someone had checked on that vehicle to make sure it was still there, and perhaps even turned it over to see if it would start. Both of these actions suggested an extended amount of surveillance, and my excitement grew as it logically fell into place. Someone in the area had to have noticed the suspicious activity around that lot in the days prior to the accident, and if I could get a good description from them I might be able to identify who these people were.

Then it wouldn't matter if they were working for the board or not. Then it wouldn't matter if Eddie Gonzalez were the sports-betting kingpin of the Panhandle. Then it wouldn't matter if my visitors intended to come back again or not.

Lester Jason, owner of Jason's Subaru, was even less pleased to see me than he'd been the first time. I'd shown the proper consideration for his customers by coming in the back way, but even so he didn't seem to want to see me.

"Look, last time was just a courtesy to Chief Tate, and the hanged truck isn't even here anymore."

"It doesn't have to be. Do you have any surveillance cameras on your lot?"

"Surveillance cameras? Mister, we're on a main drag in a busy part of town with some really good law enforcement people watching out for us. Why would I need surveillance cameras?"

It was a long shot, but I had to ask.

"Did anyone working here notice anyone paying attention to the overflow lot? Somebody asking about that truck?"

"Look, we answered these questions already, and the answer's no. You think we'd just forget to mention something like that? That vehicle was used to kill somebody, for goodness' sake! And in case you haven't noticed, this is not a truck place! We sell quality cars here. That was a trade-in, and I only wish I'd shipped it out of here sooner. Now, I'm gonna have to ask you—"

"Just one last question. Did you ever turn that SUV's engine over? Just to make sure it would start when you did move it?"

He exhaled loudly, looking at his desk. When he looked up it was with hope, though.

"You promise that's the last question?"

"Absolutely. I would like to walk around out back if you don't mind, but that's it for the questions. So how about it? You guys go out there and turn her over once in a while?"

"No need. If it doesn't fire up on moving day, we just jump it. Selling it is somebody else's problem, so we just need it to start once. And if it won't start with a jump, we flatbed it where it's going." He raised weary eyes to me. "That it?"

I walked all over that lot after that, using a disposable camera that would have ruined my chances with the fair Beth Ann Thibedault if she saw me using it. The film was extra, as most of my time was spent sketching direction and distance to the buildings nearby. I then walked all the way around every block that bordered the lot, looking for surveillance gear of any kind and coming up empty. Well, you can't get lucky every time.

Rhonda and Teddy's method of approaching my house that morning came back to me as I walked, and I began to focus on discovering just where a man in a car would sit so that he could see the SUV from the street. When Rhonda had walked up to my house, Ted had been watching her from a car a distance away, and my visitors would have done something similar for each other.

I was making the assumption that someone had walked into the lot a few nights before the event and started the truck, both to learn if it would turn over and also to practice hot-wiring it. There were no doubt more sophisticated ways of stealing the truck, but they were trying to look like amateurs and planned to dump the vehicle, so they had to do it the hard way. The guy going in would have been wearing some kind of communications rig, and the man in the car would have been watching for any trouble.

Somewhere in the back of my mind I wondered just how a grown man wearing an earphone would explain what he was doing in that lot late at night if he were in fact caught, but once again I chalked it up to overanalysis and stopped considering it. Once again I was wrong.

The canvass of the neighborhood is one of those PI things that I just hate with a passion. I would never have made it as a door-to-door salesman or a pollster, and if anything keeps me from continuing in this business, it is the distasteful chore of asking everyone in the area if they saw anything. I had been spared this on the jogging trail by the presence of camera-equipped apartment complexes, but a wise man once told me there are no shortcuts, and this time I had to do it for real.

"Excuse me, sir, I'm Frank Cole and I'm investigating the crime situation in the neighborhood. You heard that there was a sports utility vehicle stolen from Jason's Subaru over there a few weeks ago? Well, I'm looking at that theft as being part of a larger crime problem and I sure would like to get your input as someone who lives in the neighborhood."

That sounds smooth, but it really doesn't matter how polished your approach is if they don't want to talk. The key was to let them know you wanted their opinion, that you were fighting crime in their neighborhood, and that you'd listen to anything they had to say. Saying I worked for an insurance company would have definitely gotten the door slammed in my face, and since Sun Provident wasn't in any way supportive of my efforts I left them out. I did mention the Haskell agency if anyone asked, but you'd be surprised at how many people assume you're with the police or some kind of neighborhood watch organization.

My canvass wasn't limited to the stores, houses, and apartments in the area either. Hating this work as much as I do, once I get started I force myself to make careful notes and approach anyone and everyone I see. This probably wouldn't work up north, or even next door in Davis, but in Bending Palms most people would stop long enough to say they couldn't help before moving on.

I hit a long series of dead ends at first, and it was hard to keep focused on the job after giving the spiel for the tenth time and having it come to nothing. There was one bright spot where I made friends with an elderly lady by chasing away some kids with a loud car stereo, but she didn't have the foggiest idea what I was talking about even after that. It certainly took the boredom out of the day, though.

I had knocked on her front door because her house was close enough to the dealership for her to possibly see someone casing the place. It was a light green two-story home with one of those outside staircase porches that goes up to a second-story door directly over the main ground-floor entrance, and I hoped to get up on that second railing to take a gander at the overflow lot. And who knew? Maybe that upstairs door led to a makeshift apartment with a tenant who liked to go outside for a smoke late at night. The ground-floor door opened after I banged on it a second time, and I launched into my patter about protecting the neighborhood from crime.

"Thank you, but I'm not interested." The lady at the screen door said, clearly having not heard a word of my chatter and mistaking me for some kind of salesman. She was wearing a light housedress, her hair was tied up under a kerchief of some kind, and I think I had disturbed her while she was cleaning the place.

"No, ma'am, I'm not selling anything!" I tried not to yell, but she almost had the door shut, and as I said before, once I start an unpleasant job like this I get pretty ornery about finishing it. She stopped with the door half shut and gave me a hostile look.

"I said I'm not interested, young man. Now I've got some laundry to put in the dryer—" The arch words stopped as if she had been hit with high voltage, and she turned her head sharply to look over my shoulder. A weathered stockade fence marked the edge of her small yard, and a car stereo had just started blasting over it at top volume.

She muttered something that made me think the road beyond that fence was a favorite parking spot for whoever was playing that radio, and her face squinched up as if she'd bitten into a lemon. Before I gave it enough time for an intelligent decision, I saw an opening and went for it.

"Does that music bother you, ma'am?"

"Are you a policeman?" she asked hopefully, raising her voice to be heard over the din.

"No, ma'am, I'm not, but maybe I can do something about this anyway." I moved a foot backward onto one of the lower steps. "Will you talk to me when it's quieter? It's important."

"Of course."

I was several strides toward the end of the fence before I remembered that I had no idea what was on the other side of the barrier. For all I knew, this was a favorite spot for drug pushers and I was about to make the evening news the hard way. I tried in vain to come up with a plan of action, quickly discarding several crazy ideas, like pretending to be a cop. No matter how I slowed my pace, however, the end of the fence kept getting closer and closer and for the life of me I could not decide what I was going to do when I got out on the street.

It did occur to me that I could scam the old lady by offering the music people some money to go someplace else. And I certainly would have tried that, but I had less than five dollars in my wallet. My buddy Mark and his great ideas are definitely going to get me killed one of these days.

Well, you could say I was lucky. They were high schoolers parked on what turned out to be a dead-end street which backed up to the fence. They looked clean-cut enough, and there was only one car at that time of day, but the problem of making them move still remained. I stopped and stared at them, and then the solution presented itself. I was supposed to be asking questions and enlisting the aid of responsible citizens, and here were four candidates.

Two of the young men were sitting in the front seat of the car, an older sports model with one of those T-roof configurations. They were an interracial group, two white kids, one black, and one Asian, and I didn't even get halfway through my introduction when the Asian kid said something about getting away from the crazy old geezer and then they were gone, music and all.

This is the point where I am supposed to say that I had just done something stupid and dangerous, but the funny part was that this little episode gave me an idea for later use on other canvasses in other neighborhoods. I wondered if I could simply park my car out of sight, blast the music, and then come to the rescue of whomever answered the nearest door by turning off the tunes in my own car. The very notion would never have occurred to me even a week before, and I had to think that simply hanging around PIs like Haskell, Rhonda, and Teddy was rubbing off.

The old lady wasn't able to help me, but she did let me climb the outside stairs and look at a large tree that completely obstructed the view of Jason's Subaru.

There was a promising three-story building facing the lot, with stores on the bottom floor and rooms on the two floors above, and I located the manager on my second time around. He hadn't been available my first swing, but this kind of door-to-door stuff takes a lot of time and he'd returned when I came back two hours later.

His name was Henry Talbot, and he managed the upstairs rooms for the building's owners. He was a small, wiry, fifty-something with no hair and a lot of energy. He was dressed in a dull gray work shirt and black trousers, and in no time it was apparent that Henry Talbot spent every waking moment working on those two stories of apartments. He took me up to the one vacant set of rooms on the Subaru side of the building and let me look out.

"Don't get me wrong, Mr. Cole, it's nice that you're asking if we have a crime problem around here, but there's really nothing much to tell you. The town's a nice, quiet place full of families and hardworking folks. Take these rooms, for example. With the exception of Mrs. Clark, they're all young working people."

"Mrs. Clark?" I had a momentary mental picture of a shut-in with binoculars like the guy Haskell had described at the Gator Pond.

"Blind, poor dear, but we take care of her. My wife and I have the rooms right next to hers. We have her over to our place for dinner most nights, drive her to church, you know."

"I see." The luck thing was not in evidence today. "Maybe you can help me with this. I'm thinking this was an organized gang that took that truck—"

"The one that ran over that poor jogger fellow?"

"Exactly. Now these gang people, they always post lookouts, and I think they had this truck under surveillance for some time before they took it. So do you think any of your tenants might have seen somebody checking out the Subaru back lot? Somebody who lived on that side of the building?"

"Now that's smart. You've got a good head on your shoulders, son. You figure they had themselves a little look-see first, and you want us to keep an eye out for somebody like that?"

"Absolutely. But in the meantime, these folks usually develop a pattern and they stick to it, so it would be even better if someone had seen something when the truck was taken. That way we'd really know what to be looking for."

"Got it. So tell me, what do you mean when you ask if someone 'saw something'?"

For a moment there I was sure he was making fun of me, but the man's face never lost its look of expectation and I tried to answer him. It was, after all, a darn good question.

"Glad you asked. I'm thinking that they probably parked just up the street here, where the road goes uphill, so they could see into the lot itself. At first they'd just sit and look, trying to see if there was a night watchman or something."

"There is."

I dropped into one of those mental black holes where you are completely unable to form words. Henry took this as a sign that I wanted him to elaborate.

"You knew that, right? I mean, you said you talked with old Jason there. Now there's a fella who needs to take things a little easier. I'm not saying a man shouldn't work hard, but I mean he shouldn't get all fired up over every little thing."

"There's a night watchman at the Subaru dealership?"

"Sure. His name's Charlie. He lives there."

"Why didn't you tell me you have a night watchman?"

"A night watchman? You mean Charlie?" Lester Jason had seen me cutting through the service department and intercepted me, looking like a man who had had enough. As far as I was concerned, that made two of us.

"Yes. Charlie the night watchman. I asked you if you had surveillance cameras and you said there was no need because of your location and Chief Tate's wonderful police force. Why didn't you mention old Charlie as well?"

"You're interested in the truck that was stolen, right?"

"Yes!"

"Well, Charlie wasn't here that night." Lester sounded like a man talking to an ungrateful child. "Even if he was, he's just looking after the place. It's not like he patrols the grounds or anything."

"Is he here right now? May I speak with him?"

"No. As a matter of fact, I want you to leave."

We had reached an impasse of the absurd. Lester didn't know that the night of the theft was not my point of interest, and I'd just spent the entire afternoon knocking on doors and accosting people when the man who might have all the answers lived right there in the dealership. Lester and I were mirror images of misunderstanding, two sides of the same coin of stupidity. He was focused on a single night when I was looking at the evenings prior to that, and I had been covering the ground around the lot when the answer was inside it.

“Please. I’m trying to clear Eddie Gonzalez’s name so that his pregnant fiancée can get his death benefit.”

That was below the belt, for sure. Judging by the expression on his face, Lester knew the Escobars, but had been unaware that Anneliese was with child.

“Mister, if you’re lying to me—”

“I’m not. You can call Chief Dannon; I spoke to him today and he knows exactly what I’m doing.”

We stared at each other for a long moment before he softened his features.

“All right. He’s not here right now, but he comes back every night at six. You go away now and come back then, and we’ll talk to him together.” I nodded my thanks and turned to leave. “But, Mr. Cole, Charlie’s a simple guy, know what I mean? It won’t take much to upset him, and if you do that you’ll never get on this lot again.”

Upsetting Charlie Platt was the last thing I wanted to do when I met him. He was enormous.

The canvass of the neighborhood had made me work straight through lunch, and so I had eaten an early dinner at a local bar and run back to the Subaru place. Somewhere in the middle of dinner I managed to reason myself into a lower set of expectations, but I was still pretty fired up when I got into Jason’s office. Lester met me just outside.

“Listen, Charlie doesn’t know the truck was stolen, and like I said, he wasn’t even here that night, but he actually does think he’s the night watchman around here.” He seemed to be trying to say something. “The truth is he’s a little slow, but he’s a really sweet guy, and if he heard that something got taken off the lot he’d be heartbroken.”

“Got it.” I nodded while coming up with a different approach. “I’ll tell him I’m looking for someone who might have been hanging around the neighborhood a few weeks ago. I won’t mention the truck.”

“Okay, but I gotta warn you, he’s not real clear on calendar things. Three weeks ago, three months ago, they’re pretty meaningless to him.”

That didn’t sound encouraging.

Charlie was seated in front of Lester’s desk, and the two of them had been enjoying a couple of burgers and sodas. Charlie looked up from his chair with a child’s eyes. His hair was cut almost marine-style, and he wore one of the service area’s gray one-piece pullovers. It had the name “Charlie” embroidered on the left chest, and it reminded me of the service station shirt Rosie Gonzalez had been wearing when we had talked. The one-piece was spotless, and Charlie wore a set of spit-shined black shoes with athletic socks. He was probably forty.

“Charlie just came back from his job at the courthouse,” Lester said proudly as he steered me toward the big man. “Charlie sweeps up for Judge Harris, don’t you, Charlie?”

“Every day, rain or shine,” he said in a singsong, smiling brightly. The pressure of Lester’s hand on my arm increased substantially, and I nodded at him to show I understood. Charlie had gone back to eating, and I sat down in an empty folding chair next to him.

“Hi, Charlie. My name is Frank.”

“Hi, Frank. How do you do?” He had politely returned the half-eaten burger to the paper plate before looking me in the eyes again. Someone had taught him to do that, and to say those words.

“I’m fine, Charlie.” I made myself relax, feeling that the usual question-and-answer routine was going to have to take a backseat here. “You work for Judge Harris?”

“Judge Harris is really smart, Frank. He’s the most important man in the building.”

“I’ll bet he is.” I looked at Lester, and he spoke from behind the desk.

“Charlie, Frank has been looking around our neighborhood here.”

“Frank, are you going to move here?” Charlie asked this in an excited voice, and although I wasn't sure if he meant Bending Palms or the blocks immediately adjacent to the lot, I could tell that Charlie considered "here" to be a very good place.

"Actually, Charlie, I was looking for a friend of mine who was here a few weeks ago." I had no idea how to orient his thinking to several weeks before. Maybe he was a sports fan, in which case I could do some checking about the teams he watched.

"Frank, if you're looking for someone, you should ask a police officer." Someone had taught him that one as well. I continued quietly.

"They might not have seen him, Charlie. He came to this neighborhood at night, and he would have been right around here, probably sitting in his car."

"Charlie doesn't really go out at night much, Frank—"

"I saw him. I saw your friend."

I didn't respond to that, largely because I had come to the conclusion that Charlie was not going to be of any help. He clearly got around well enough on his own, going back and forth to his job at the courthouse, but it sounded more like he lived at the dealership than looked after the place. Lester saved the day, speaking calmly.

"Who did you see, Charlie? Was he in a car?"

"Yes, Lester. It was the night the fire engines went by. I went out to look at them."

"Frank, there was a fire on the other side of town a month ago. You told me about it the next day, didn't you, Charlie?"

"Yes, Lester." He was reliving the excitement, and his chair squeaked as he moved around. "The fire trucks went right by our house. I heard them even though I had the TV on. And I went outside to see them."

I guessed he referred to the dealership as "our house," but the timing of the fire, a week or so before the accident, suggested that he might just have seen one of the bad guys scoping out the lot.

"Where was the man, Charlie?"

"You mean your friend, Frank?"

"Yes, my friend. Where was he? Was he walking around?"

"No, he was in his car." He turned in his seat and pointed out the back maintenance bay door where the street went uphill. Exactly where someone looking into the lot would sit. "I went up there because I could see better. It's a hill. You can see better from a hill."

"Did you talk to him?"

"Yes, Frank. I asked him if he saw the fire trucks go by, and he said he did."

"Charlie, can you tell me what he looked like?"

"Yes, Frank. Yes, I can."

I leaned forward unconsciously, waiting for the words. "What did he look like, Charlie?"

"He looked just like me."

It took some time to determine that Charlie simply meant the man in the car was big. Lester let me narrow that down some more by asking yes-and-no questions (Was he black? Did he have a mustache?—you get the idea), and I ended up with a dark-haired, clean-shaven Caucasian in a business suit. That might not sound like much, but I got the impression that if I showed Charlie a picture of this man he would remember him. And since the guy was sounding like one of the ones who had followed me on the highway, there was a slim chance I might get a picture at some point. Or maybe Rhonda and Teddy would.

Thinking of Haskell's people made me ask to use Lester's phone, and Rhonda seemed pleased to hear from me when she answered. Apparently Haskell had some new information and had called asking where I was. Charlie had already gone off to his room, and I stayed behind to apologize to Lester.

"I'm sorry I was such a pain, Lester. And I have to say I misjudged you. You're one heck of a nice guy."

"It's not just me, Frank. Judge Harris and his bailiffs basically adopted Charlie a long time ago, but you can see he's pretty independent. They wanted him to have a place of his own within walking distance of the courthouse. The whole town knows Charlie. That's why I was upset by that busybody Talbot saying he was our night watchman. He knows better than that."

"Lester, I don't know who this phantom stranger was, but if I get some possible candidates, can I show Charlie some pictures?"

"Judge Harris would tell you that wouldn't hold up in court."

"It doesn't have to. If I can find out who was scoping out your lot and your truck, I'll just stay on the guy until I get something that *will* hold up in court." I stuck out my hand, and Lester took it.

"It wasn't my truck, Frank. I told you, we sell cars here."

Charlie's story sounded awfully lame when I relayed it to Haskell, but maybe that was because Rhonda and Teddy were sitting there listening. They had unpacked some of their superspy stuff, which was now laid out on my living room floor, but I had to suspect they did that when they learned their boss was going to swing by.

"See what I told you, gang? Frank's a natural." I don't know how Rhonda or Ted felt, but Haskell seemed to think I'd found something. "Me, I wouldn't have ever gone back to that car lot or even that jogging path. But Frank here did, and he began walking around in slowly increasing circles until he found something."

Rhonda managed to keep a straight face, but Ted seemed on the verge of laughing. I wasn't sure if they felt Haskell was snowing me or if they had heard that sermon once too often, but their boss continued.

"In the meantime we now have two people who could ID at least one of the people involved here. Frank played heads-up ball with the guys tailing him and got a good look at one of them, and this Charlie can probably narrow down our list of suspects. Good job."

Haskell and I were sitting at the tiny kitchen table that had come with the house, Rhonda was sitting on the counter by the sink, and Ted filled the doorway leading back into the living room. Haskell had brought them pizza, and it was a lucky thing I had already eaten because three empty boxes now sat on my coffee table.

"Okay. Speaking of a suspect list, I've been busy myself." Haskell was dressed in some kind of yachting outfit, off-white pants with boat shoes, a blue shirt, maroon tie, and a blue blazer with a nautical crest on the pocket. "I was down in Tampa this morning—"

"Tampa? What's in Tampa?"

Haskell smiled, enjoying his role as mentor and manager.

"If we want dirt on somebody, where do we go, gang?"

"To the competition." Rhonda and Teddy spoke in unison, but without enthusiasm.

"That's right. You see, Frank, we could infiltrate the country club scene in Davis, but we'd find out absolutely nothing about the Hayward board because they're big fish in that particular pond. Even people who don't like them have to live in that pond, and they wouldn't take a chance that what they said would get back to the Hayward people.

"And as much as the caddies and the waiters probably know everything there is to know about Mr. Hurst and his cronies, the same thing applies.

"So if you really want dirt, go to someone who can benefit from telling it to you."

"Frank already knows that, Bill. He's divorced." Teddy spoke playfully from the door, and Haskell's face squinched up for a moment.

"You're divorced? You never told me that."

"What I get for letting total strangers into my house."

Haskell didn't stay off track for long. He took a notebook out of his coat pocket.

"Anyway, Hayward's big competition is down in Tampa, and believe me they're not happy about Hayward getting sold to that Venezuelan outfit. Apparently they've kept the really big players out of here for decades and this is going to be a major problem for them." He flipped a couple of pages.

"I won't bore you with the standard stuff, the wild parties and the car wrecks. Even if it's true it's immaterial. But here's the guy that caught my eye. Sanford Hurst the Fourth or Fifth or whatever he is, he's the CFO's son, and he's a beaut." Haskell had done a little Web surfing himself, it seemed, as he dropped a color facsimile printout on the table showing the mug shot of an unkempt teenager. It was impossible to tell how tall he was, but his tousled hair was light brown, his eyes were blue, and he looked like he was getting ready to lead a prison break.

"I read about him. He left for Europe a couple of weeks ago."

"That's him. This picture was taken two years ago, and it wasn't the first time he'd been pulled in. The kid's got a history of not playing well with others. Apparently his dad has had to pay hush money all up and down the coast. And get this: Our boy here is a compulsive car thief."

"Car thieves know how to hot-wire SUVs." Rhonda spoke from the counter.

"Yes, they do. And his dad has been quite vocal about his opposition to the sale of Hayward Shipping."

"So we have motive," Teddy said quietly, with a distant look in his eyes that suggested he was putting the puzzle together pretty fast.

"Yes, we do. Unhappy family, loss of income, maybe even loss of inheritance, take your pick. And since his old man is CFO, the kid doesn't have to be a genius to see that running over Spector would put the world back on its axis again."

It was all moving too fast for me, but I was uncomfortable challenging these three. No doubt Haskell had waded through a dozen other stories of rehab and embezzlement and discarded every one of them for some reason or other. He had seized on this one, though, and it did seem to fit.

"Um, I'm the new guy here, so this is just a thought. The guys who did this weren't thrill seekers. They put a lot of thought into constructing a murder that wouldn't get investigated, one where they'd have very little chance of getting identified in the act or caught getting away. They watched that SUV for days or even weeks before deciding to use it. I just don't see this kid fitting that."

Contrary to my expectations, no one ridiculed me. Rhonda looked at the linoleum floor, Teddy bit his lower lip, and even Haskell looked as if he were at least considering what I said before he answered.

"That's a good point, Frank, but we've always gone off of the idea that he wasn't acting alone. The guy you saw, and the guy this Charlie saw, was a big guy in a suit, not this kid obviously. In the meantime they had to have some kind of getaway car to use after dumping the SUV—"

"Coulda prepositioned that. One guy could have done this alone if he already put the car there," Teddy offered.

"That's true, but the driver still had to get to the lot and steal the truck. Somebody took him there."

"Not if he stole the truck the night before," Rhonda said from behind Haskell, shooting an impish look at Teddy. Haskell took the bait.

"Yes, it is true that they could have prepositioned the car." He sounded exasperated, and the other two couldn't contain their smiles. He didn't see what was going on behind him, and I fixed him with a look of utmost seriousness. "But why? We already know that somebody, somebody who doesn't look like this kid, was tailing Frank and probably staking out the lot. Are you saying they watched the lot for a week while sitting in a car up the street, but made the driver hoof it there on the big night?"

Teddy burst out laughing, and Rhonda joined in at a lower volume. Not sure of the protocol, I only smiled at Bill until he saw that they were having some fun with him. He threw a few choice words at them and then continued when the laughter had abated.

"Sometimes I wonder why I bother. At any rate, we've got enough to go start asking questions at Hayward Shipping. I called Spector in New York and he's told Mr. Hurst to be available. Two of the others are going to be there tomorrow, too, so we won't be tipping our hand right off." He was looking straight at me as he spoke.

"That's right, Frank. *We.* Get a good night's sleep, because tomorrow you and I are walking right into the hornet's nest. They seemed to think they could waltz in here and drop off that message, so now we'll see how comfortable they are when you do the same thing."

"And what message are we supposed to be dropping off?"

"You're the message, Frank."

CHAPTER EIGHT

In my opinion, this investigation had run into a brick wall. Logic pointed toward the Hayward Shipping board as containing the culprits, but it was by no means a lock. Spector had confided to Haskell that harsh words had passed between him and Hurst, and the sudden emigration of Hurst's wayward son certainly looked suspicious, but it was not a lot to go on. In the meantime there was the danger that Haskell had pointed out at the beginning, the possibility that this was the reaction of a psycho pipefitter with military training or some other complete unknown. To my inexperienced eyes, this looked like a set of facts that might not actually lead where we thought they did, and even if our summations were correct we really had no proof.

Hayward Shipping's financial statements and business reputation all said it was a well-run company, and that impression was reinforced when we got to their corporate headquarters. Their entire management area amounted to a single building with three floors of offices down near the docks. The air smelled of sea salt, and enormous shipping cranes could be seen from the windows. Despite its age and size, this was still a lean and mean organization, still oriented on the business and dedicated to keeping the overhead low.

This was not to say that their offices were shabby. On the contrary, every inch of the building was carpeted or paneled, wall-sized laser art depicted old-style ships at sea or hardy dockworkers plying their trade, and the place was a beehive of activity. As my own business had not lasted long enough to be the target of a merger, I could only assume this was what a head office looked like when the new owners were taking over.

Haskell and I had parked his Mustang at the end of a long line of Mercedes and BMWs, and we walked by a massive anchor that had been converted into some kind of modern art in front of the building. We had been checked onto the dock by a Hayward security guard, and Haskell had already arranged for us to be met in the lobby by Spector's personal assistant, a comely blonde named Denise. For all her looks, Denise had clearly been left behind to mind the store in what was very much an anti-Spector atmosphere. She was a pivotal element in our little charade that morning, and Haskell had spent a fair amount of time on the phone with her the night before.

"Mr. Haskell, Mr. Cole, I'm pleased to meet you," she said for the benefit of the security man at the reception desk. Denise wore a smart pink jacket-and-skirt business outfit, her hair was pulled up in a bun behind her head, and I put her down in my book as being harder than a coffin nail. "Shall we?"

We took the open central stairs up to the third floor, where the top management offices were located. A brunette version of Denise greeted us perfunctorily and told Denise that Mr. Hurst was in. She gave off a vibration that suggested she was not a member of the Spector faction at Hayward Shipping, and when I smiled at her, I thought she was going to throw something at me. Haskell had conspired with Denise the night before to make certain that I was with him when he was introduced to Hurst, and so the three of us simply stood by the unfriendly secretary while she intercommed into the corridor behind her to let the CFO know his ten o'clock was there.

Hurst came out himself. He was accompanied by a man who was either a personal assistant or a lawyer. Both men wore dark suits and bright ties.

Hurst was a tall, lean man with a thin ring of gray hair connecting his ears. He had a look of intelligence. His eyes were a deep blue, and he looked like a guy who could play thirty-six holes of golf without breaking a sweat. The other man was average height, brown hair, slightly pudgy but in a self-satisfied, affluent way that suggested he had so much money that he didn't need to be fit. Hurst walked right up, and Haskell went right back into his imitation of a career diplomat. He was dressed in a dark gray double-breasted while I was still wearing my Boy Friday getup.

"Mr. Hurst, thanks so much for taking time out of your schedule to see me."

"Of course. Drew sounded more than a little concerned about this, so anything I can do to set his mind at ease." He let that sentence drop off as he turned those eyes toward mine. Perhaps he was one of those public relations types who kisses every baby within a mile of them, but I got the impression that he was memorizing my face as he stuck out his hand and I shook it. "And you are . . ."

"Frank Cole, sir, I work with Bill."

"Frank's the one who noticed the similarity between Mr. Spector and the accident victim," Bill offered proudly, gauging the reaction of both men. He had been almost completely honest when requesting this meeting, telling Hurst about Eddie Gonzalez and the various coincidences that had brought us to Hayward Shipping. Instead of suggesting that he considered any board members possible suspects, though, he had suggested that Hurst could help us by identifying dissatisfied elements within the company who might harbor ill will against the CEO.

"He's got no place to go on that one," Bill had explained to me. "Either he knows nothing, in which case he'll view this as another sign that they picked a wimp for CEO, or he knows a lot, in which case he'll want to pretend to cooperate. He may even try to send us off on a false scent, but more than likely I won't get anything from him."

"Very nice to meet you, Mr. Cole. I'm sure Drew appreciates your concern." It was the second time he'd mentioned Spector's name and the word "concern" in the same sentence, and it became obvious that he was seriously undermining his current boss. Just discussing this in front of the receptionist was probably unwise, but he was speaking loudly and I suspected that everyone in the building knew that their CEO was seeing shadows. Hurst released his grip and swung a hand at waist level toward his companion. "This is our corporate counsel, David Haller. I thought he might be able to help us in our discussion."

As Haller stepped up I could only marvel at Haskell's understanding of these people. He'd predicted that Hurst would manage to get a lawyer in the room when they talked. While still shaking Haller's hand, Bill turned to Denise.

"I'm sorry, Denise, why don't you take Frank and get started while I speak with Mr. Hurst?" He had already taken a step toward Hurst, as if to sweep him back down the hall toward his office, but the CFO was a quick one. He kept the same bland smile as he tried to understand this strange development.

"Is this something I could help you with?" he asked, looking straight at me. I didn't need to act to look away, bringing my eyes to Denise's as if caught with my hand in the cookie jar. I had rehearsed that reaction with Haskell the night before.

"Oh, it's nothing, Mr. Hurst," she said. "Drew asked me to give

Mr. Haskell access to his appointment book and Frank is going to look at that with me." She should have been in Hollywood.

"You know, the appointment book, address book, phone log, anything that might be related." Bill spoke up, his lines well practiced and cool. He dropped the bomb while speaking like a proud father. "Frank's a real bloodhound on this stuff. Sees things most of us don't. Shall we?"

The Academy Award would still go to Hurst, though, as he leaned over to the woman at the reception desk.

"Natalie, make my records available to Mr. Cole as well." He looked right through me for a second. "Maybe we can put this bloodhound on the right trail and set Drew's mind to rest."

Spector's office, sporting a modest black sign announcing his name and title, was directly across from Hurst's. The whole building suggested a different era in American business, before e-mails and cell phones, when the top manager and the top finance guy sat facing each other with their desks pressed together. It was how I'd run my company, except the desk facing mine had been my office manager's, and, believe me, you can cut down on the paperwork when all you have to do is look up and ask for facts or a decision.

Spector's office was a lot like Haskell's in Tallahassee. The only difference was a portable putting green set up in the middle of the carpet. Denise walked over to Spector's desk and began tapping at the keyboard while speaking to Natalie on the intercom.

"Go ahead and link Mr. Hurst's office secretary into this PC. We'll take it from there." She smiled at me sweetly, no doubt enjoying whatever reaction she was getting from the Hurst loyalist on the other end of the line. Even if we were completely on the wrong track here, the civil war in Hayward Shipping was going to be interesting to watch.

Denise sat me down at the desk and quickly identified the various windows she had popped up on the screen. Although I was going to go through the motions of scrutinizing Spector's appointments, Haskell's main purpose was to have me look at all the pictures in Hayward's personnel files. Of course, there wouldn't be a photo of every employee, but Bill didn't expect me to see anyone I would recognize anyway. The whole thing was a ruse, as Denise had assured us that every screen I viewed would be retrieved by Hurst's people later that day. That is, if dear Natalie hadn't piped the view straight to a Hurst henchman in another part of the building already.

In addition to looking at the personnel photos, I was supposed to peruse an extensive archive containing the company's internal newsletter and its various community activities. The newsletter and the feel-good stuff would be jammed with photographs of Hayward people planting trees, handing out checks, and receiving awards. Anyone monitoring my activities would become convinced that I had a picture or a sketch of someone involved in the killing of Eddie Gonzalez.

This is not as far-fetched as it might sound. Spector had sprung the sale of Hayward Shipping on its board only two weeks prior to Eddie Gonzalez's death. The vote had taken place a few days later, and the Hurst faction had probably felt secure in their one-vote advantage over Spector's people. The vote had gone unexpectedly wrong, and so there had been little cause for backup plans before then. That had left the plotters, presumably button-down businessmen without paid assassins waiting in the outer office, very little time to rig up their little accident. It was highly unlikely that they had gone to strangers, and so the possibility that they had used a trusted subordinate (or the insane son of the CFO) was not out of the question.

In the meantime, I had gotten a look at one of the guys tailing me days before, and he might just be in one of these stored pictures. I also had a moderately good description from Charlie, the Subaru night watchman, of a big man who had been casing the dealership a few nights before the event, and I was going to print off close-ups of anyone who fit that model to show to Charlie later. I was also going to print off a random assortment of shots to confuse anyone watching my computer play, and it was hard to resist running off a shot of the smiling Mr. Sanford Hurst from the company's annual report. Haskell had warned me not to do that simply because guys like Sanford Hurst are never close enough to the action to be identified by any of the culprits, but it amused me to think it might wipe that smile off the guy's face.

At any rate, reviewing those pictures was a lot like looking at home movies of total strangers doing absolutely nothing, and after I thought I'd done it long enough I wandered back out to the hallway and into Denise's office one door down. She was running a similar check of personnel records, confidential stuff that I couldn't look at without causing a fuss, no matter who the CEO was. She looked up with an evil sneer while speaking for the benefit of anyone listening.

"Hi, Frank. How are things coming along?"

"Great." I leaned in to whisper in her ear, and the scent of her perfume reminded me of the promised date with Beth Ann at Farragut College when this sordid business was over. "Any chance that Sanford junior is in any of these pictures?"

Both Bill and I had forgotten to mention the kid to Denise, which was understandable when you remember he was not an employee.

"Sure," she whispered back, tapping a few commands to search the public relations stuff for the kid's name. It returned a million lines because he shared the same name with the company's CFO, but she was computer savvy and narrowed the search quickly. "We've got the archives heavily cross-indexed so that we can highlight by a single department or an individual's name. It makes it easier to assemble a quick biography when someone is getting promoted or when there's a media inquiry."

The screen jumped, and a gang of teenagers surrounding a gleaming sports car appeared.

"This was a car wash run by the employees' kids a year ago. They donated the money to a local group that buys wheelchairs for the indigent." She pointed to a tall figure in the back of the group. "That's him."

The scene was classic Americana, with about twenty teens in wet bathing suits waving and smiling in the rays of a bright sunny day, posing around one of the finished products of their handiwork. The tousled hair of Sanford Hurst's namesake rose above a handsome young face that seemed to be laughing at something someone had just said.

"Great," I thought. "A car wash. Exactly where you want a troubled kid with a penchant for grand theft auto." He was probably laughing because he'd spotted the next set of wheels he was going to boost.

Sprinkled through the back rank of car washers was a set of grown-ups who were probably there to keep the adolescent horseplay from getting too far out of hand. Next to Sandy Hurst stood a massive older man, his biceps bulging inside a dark T-shirt that made me notice he had his arm around the laughing boy's shoulders. The big man's lips had been moving when the picture was taken, and the kid had been laughing at whatever he was saying.

"Who's this big guy?" I asked, still keeping my voice low and pointing.

"Oh, that's Marty Stone, head of security. He's a super guy, always wanted to send someone with Drew when he went jogging on that trail, but Drew wouldn't let him."

"He close with the kid?"

"Very." She leaned closer, conspiratorial. "Drew brought me with him when he got the CEO job, so I haven't been here that long, but from what I understand, Marty practically raised that kid."

Denise had given me directions to Martin Stone's office, so I just walked right by Natalie the receptionist on my way to the other end of the third floor. I didn't know if Stone would be in or not, and I wasn't sure I wanted to confront him anyway, but something made me leave the computer stuff behind and go for a real live conversation.

Natalie did try to stop me, but under the thin guise that I was not allowed to simply wander the building. I murmured something about Mr. Spector giving us his approval to talk to anyone we wanted to and kept moving.

I crossed the staircase landing and moved into what was presumably security territory. Somewhere in the back of my mind I was seeing a chance encounter with one of the men who had tailed me, complete with the startled face and maybe even followed by a panicky flight. The folks we were pursuing would have to be pretty stupid for that man to be in the building with me at the same time, but I did hold a small hope and looked through every open office door.

There were a lot of open doors, which suggested again that Hayward Shipping was probably a pretty good place to work. People smiled at me as they passed in the hallway, and the open doors led into the offices of some of the more senior corporate officers. The door with Martin Stone's name above it was likewise open, and to my astonishment the big man was sitting at his desk talking on the phone. He looked up from behind a standard wood desk, and when we made eye contact he excused himself to whoever was on the other end of the line and asked, "Hi, may I help you?" I would have sworn he didn't know who I was.

I raised a hand in greeting and suggested he could finish his conversation, saying I was in no hurry but frantically trying to decide how to proceed. He waved me in and pointed toward a chair, but I took the opportunity to check out the many framed pictures hanging on the facing wall. I was thinking fast and looking for anything showing Sanford junior, and I did make out a picture of Stone in some kind of police uniform with a group of cops, a newspaper story in which Stone and his security people had thwarted a drug ring attempting to infiltrate Hayward, and a good citizenship award or two. No pictures of the kid, though.

He hung up, stood, and extended a giant paw. As my hand disappeared inside his I saw a picture of the kid right there on the desk. As I sat down I looked hard at him for any sign of discomfort and found none. Stone was probably six foot four, easily two hundred and fifty pounds, and none of it was fat. His eyes were green, and his buzz cut was brown, turning gray.

"Yes, Mr. Hurst said Mr. Spector had brought in some outside investigators on a personal matter. I'm glad you dropped by. As security chief I'm sure I'm in a position to help you out with any questions you might have."

"Thanks a lot. I don't know how much they told you, but we're investigating a possible connection between a hit-and-run on the same jogging trail that Mr. Spector uses and Mr. Spector himself. The accident victim could have been mistaken for Mr. Spector, and since the victim had no enemies we were concerned enough to contact your CEO."

"Yes, I'm aware of that. Mr. Hurst told me."

"I was just talking to Mr. Spector's personal assistant—" I flipped open my notebook as if searching for her name.

"Denise."

"Yes, Denise. She said you had suggested that the CEO take some security along during his nightly runs but that he didn't agree. Was that just precautionary or did you think someone might want to harm Mr. Spector?"

"If I thought the trail was dangerous I would not have let him out there alone," Stone replied evenly, but an edge crept into his voice. It was hard to tell if he were insulted by the question or simply speaking as the man in charge of security. "No, Frank, working with high-powered people like we have here at Hayward, you have to recognize that they're in the public eye a lot. Anything from a disgruntled employee to a save-the-whales type might have accosted Mr. Spector, so that was what really concerned me."

"Do the other company officers take their security more seriously?"

"Mr. Hurst does, but he's from an old-money family."

"I'm new to this business, so you'll have to forgive me for a little ignorance. Does that mean—"

"It means he grew up with security people around him all the time. It's a way of life for him and his family."

"I noticed you have a picture of his son on your desk. Are you part of his family's security?"

He reached over and picked up the small frame. He looked at it with a mix of affection and concern, and for the very first time I had a gut feeling that I was on the right track. Nothing concrete, mind you, but a definite impression. He handed the picture across and continued in the same loose, friendly fashion.

"No, I'm closer to him than that. My job here wouldn't allow me to supervise the family protection anyway." He leaned closer and lowered his voice. "You have to understand that Mr. Hurst is a very busy man. He's got thousands of people working for him, and, unfortunately, taking care of all of them sometimes shortchanges his family.

"But he does care, and over time he's handpicked a few people like myself to be there for Sandy. When Sandy was younger it was mostly tutors, but when he became a teenager Mr. Hurst asked me to start doing things with him. Physical fitness, role modeling, you know. Sometimes just being there for the kid to talk to is enough."

I almost asked about Sandy's brushes with the law, but Haskell saved me from blowing the whole case and probably getting beat up by a guy twice my size. He poked his head in the door and said brightly, "Oh, there you are. Natalie said you wandered off down in this direction."

He walked in with that hand-reaching arm extended and shook Stone's hand before the other man could rise from his chair. "Bill Haskell, Haskell Investigations—" A business card was magically placed in Stone's hand. "I was just speaking with Mr. Hurst while Frank was looking at Mr. Spector's recent appointments."

"Yes. I know." Stone's response to Haskell was markedly different from the reception he'd given me. A full second elapsed between the first and second syllables of his response, and his voice was sharp. He sounded like a brain surgeon who has just been told that hemorrhaging and bleeding mean the same thing. It was not the first time that I had seen professional investigators mock Haskell's salesman act, and it occurred to me that the chief of Hayward security might already know of Haskell Investigations. "Frank and I were just discussing the security considerations common to the senior officers here."

"Excellent. I'm sure Frank asked you this, but did Mr. Spector take his protection seriously?"

"After the merger was announced there were death threats, so we added some of my guys to the CEO's personal security. Until then there really wasn't anything to worry about, apart from the usual threats to rich people."

"Yes, I saw the extra guys when we visited Mr. Spector at his home the other day. So his normal security wasn't provided by Hayward?"

I kept a blank face while waiting for the answer. Stone had given me the impression that his only knowledge of our involvement came from the briefing Hurst had given him. However, if the augmentees we had seen at Spector's place were actually some of Stone's people, you can bet they told their chief that strange PIs were in town.

"Yes, the corporation does not provide personal protection for the families except in work-related cases, or travel to high-risk parts of the world."

"I can imagine. Your guys go to South America a lot?" Haskell had gotten whatever he was looking for and was moving Stone off the topic.

"Not any more than we can help. Corporate abduction is practically a tradition in some of these countries."

"So I've heard." He turned to me. "Frank, we're going to have to come back when more members of the board are available. Nice meeting you." He shook Stone's hand again and we were out the door.

"Frank, you've done some really good things on your own for this investigation, but I have got to ask you to cool it." We were driving back toward Exile with the top down so he had to shout. "What were you thinking, confronting Stone like that?"

"It wasn't a confrontation." I paused for a moment. "In fact, I'm not sure what it was. He fits the description of the guy who was casing the Subaru dealership, but Denise said he was always after Spector not to go jogging alone."

"That's his job, Frank. He's the security guy."

"Yes, he is. But he's also playing Big Brother to Hurst's kid, the one with the car-theft problem who just suddenly decided to go to Europe for a few years. According to Denise he practically raised Sandy junior."

That was an important piece of information we had not known just a day earlier, and Haskell gave it some thought before replying.

"Did you ask him about that?"

"Yeah, but he gave me the press conference answer, about how Hurst senior has to look out for the welfare of all the employees and doesn't have time for his family."

"Perfect."

"What?"

"You are a gem, Frank. You asked him about his relationship to the kid?"

"Yes."

"Well, who knows? You might have just moved us a big distance down the road."

"How do you mean?"

"Well, as expected I didn't get anything from Hurst senior. So you can bet they're going over every keystroke you punched in on Spector's PC even as we speak. Just like we planned, they're gonna figure we have a witness to something they did, and if they add in your question about the kid they might just do something stupid."

"Like putting a bullet on my kitchen table, or maybe firing it this time?"

"That's not going to happen. There are far too many people in the equation now. No, I mean something stupid like sending the kid to Europe when nobody was asking about him. That was a dead giveaway. And now there's a chance the head of security was involved."

"I don't think so. He doesn't come across that way."

"Are you crazy? He fits perfectly. You said it yourself, these guys were pros. They planned it, did reconnaissance, and when you got nosy they tried to scare you off without letting you know who they were."

"But would a guy who wanted to assign extra security turn around one hundred eighty degrees and murder his boss? This guy Stone has duty and loyalty written all over him."

"You said it. Duty and loyalty. Duty to what, and loyalty to whom? His duty is to Hayward Shipping, which just turned into a small subsidiary of a giant multinational in an entirely different country. And his loyalty seems tilted an awful lot toward the Hurst family, who at the very least watched the family business get sold by a Yankee that Hurst senior helped put in charge.

"Now throw in the kid. He steals cars for fun. Even if he walked straight into an FBI sting in that overflow lot while boosting that SUV, who's gonna think anything is out of the ordinary? This is what he does for kicks. But if you catch the head of security for Hayward Shipping driving a stolen SUV, or in the act of stealing it, you've got a whole bunch of unpleasant questions to answer.

"He's perfect, Frank. Perfect."

We went back to my house, where Rhonda and Teddy were waiting. They hadn't been there all day, having been dispatched that morning with instructions to dig into Sanford junior's criminal record. This was one of those areas where Internet fact-checking and perusal of court documents would get you nowhere, and the two PIs had used an extensive network of friends to give them the information they sought.

I didn't bother questioning the legality of this sort of work, but since almost every one of the kid's transgressions had been swept under the rug, I had to wonder just how wrong it could be. With my own ongoing legal problems, you can bet I never went anywhere near that line, but it seemed clear that Rhonda and Ted were comfortable in that judicial no-man's-land.

"Kid reminds me of me," Rhonda announced from the kitchen table, where she was deftly manipulating a pair of chopsticks in a carton of Chinese takeout. With all the sitting around and all the junk food, you had to wonder how she and Ted stayed in such good shape. "Never met a car he didn't like. Not that he tries to run off with every set of wheels he comes across, but it's close.

"Anyway, we talked to some cops down in Preston—"

"Well, not just Preston." Teddy spoke up from his spot on my couch, where he was devouring the second of two submarine sandwiches. "Every one of these places led to another one. That kid is pretty busy."

"Yeah, but Preston was the one where we got some real good stuff. Apparently the deputy who booked him—"

"They booked him?" This was from Bill, who was pacing back and forth in my living room with his tie off. I was not familiar enough with the justice system to know whether booking is routine, but I guess it isn't. I knew the kid had gone to court on at least one of these offenses, though, and had to assume that he had gone through the formal process of booking at the time.

"Yeah, he got booked that once, but it was early in his career. Now it seems that the local law up and down the coast knows the drill when it comes to this kid. You know, the kid's underage, this Stone guy shows up and smooths things over, and before you know it, *whoosh*"—she blew air across an open palm—"the booking records are just part of some flatfoot's private collection."

"Stone himself came and got him?"

"Every time. No matter when or where. What, did you meet him?"

"Frank did." Bill gave me an odd look, as if he were deciding whether to recommend me for a Nobel Prize or have me burned as a witch. "Go on."

"Well, you know the drill. Hurst has more money than the Federal Reserve, his family's superpowerful, and according to the cops we talked to, this Stone is a very smooth guy. Comes on light even though he's a big boy, used to be a cop, talks the talk with the guys in uniform, and he walks out with the kid."

"Except in Bending Palms." Teddy spoke quietly, the voice of Rhonda's memory.

"Yeah. Chief Tate doesn't play these games, even though everybody in law enforcement knows about the kid by then. So he's still a juvenile, it got pulled up in front of a judge, but it got dismissed." Rhonda paged through a small spiral-bound notebook.

"Clerk said the judge really chewed the kid out good, but with the kind of lawyers the family brought in, that was all he could do." Teddy stepped in, talking while stuffing the wrappings from his lunch into a small trash bin that usually sat in my bathroom.

"Right. Some technicality. But Tate had already told us that the kid seemed to get the message. Either he's gotten really good at not getting caught or he's gone back to shop class where he belongs."

"Shop class?"

"Yeah, that's what the deputy in Preston told us. Turns out this deputy sat with the kid for a few hours waiting for Stone, and they're both car nuts. He said the kid's bright enough, knows his engines, and that the kid said his folks hadn't wanted him taking shop classes like basic engine repair."

"Sanford senior couldn't bear the thought of his namesake rubbing elbows with the grease monkeys," Bill murmured, still pacing. "How about when Stone showed up? Any of the people you talked to say what the kid's reaction was?"

"Yeah, a couple of them. They all noticed that the kid played it right when he got caught, that he didn't give them lip and seemed to know he'd get away clean, but a couple of the cops said that he really brightened up when he saw Stone." Rhonda flipped a page and read a quotation. " 'Me, if my old man had been called down to the station to get me at that age I would have begged the cops to keep me, but the kid seemed to really like Mr. Stone.' "

There was a silence while Bill thought that one over, so I asked something that had popped into my head.

"Rhonda, you're gonna have to forgive my ignorance here, but how did the kid know where Stone was? He have a toll number or something?"

Rhonda and Ted exchanged smiles before she answered.

"They're not supposed to let people know this, but some stations keep a record of who you call for help. The number's the same every time that we got them to share that with us. Sounds like Stone's personal cell."

"This goes back some years?"

"Yeah, two." Rhonda considered my question and brightened when she saw where I was going. "Mr. Stone has kept the same number for a while, hasn't he?"

Bill didn't see it at first. "That was the panic number for Sandy junior. They'd pay big bucks to keep the same one. No way they'd take the chance that he couldn't get through to Stone."

"Naw, Bill. The kid could always call home and they'd get somebody out there. I think Frank's pointing out that Sanford senior couldn't be bothered."

Actually, that wasn't what I was onto, but it made sense and pushed Stone and the kid a little closer together. If Sanford junior had conceived a diabolical plan to murder his father's tormentor, the one man he'd share it with would be Stone. And maybe Stone had gone along to make sure nothing happened to the boy he'd spent so much time babysitting.

I dropped off the kitchen counter. It was still light out, but I wasn't sure just how much longer Harvey Webster would be at work.

"I'm going out for a while. Where are you going to be?"

Bill didn't seem to notice. He wore a troubled expression that was very far out of character, and it looked as if he had decided that he had the right man but couldn't prove it.

"Where are you going?"

"I have a couple of questions for Harvey over at Sun Provident."

"Thought you quit them."

"I did. Just tying up a loose end or two."

"Okay." He turned to Teddy. "Ted, go with him. Make sure nobody gives him trouble. Rhonda and I are going to run down some more information on Mr. Stone."

"I don't think there's any need to waste Teddy's time like that."

"You got tailed when this started, and you shook them when you went into hiding. Well, today you stuck your thumb right in

Sanford senior's eye, so who knows what may happen? Take Teddy with you."

The big man came up on his feet as if by magic, and we headed for the door. It was odd that Bill had remembered my experience with the people who had tailed me, but had not seen where I was headed with this. He was the one who had decided that Barstow had set the tail on me when we met at Harvey's office, but he didn't make the guess that Barstow might have used Harvey's phone to call my friends in the tan car.

If Barstow used Harvey's phone, I could check that number and see if he called the same cell phone that Sanford junior dialed every time he got hauled in by the police. And if that number matched, we had a direct link between the people who tailed me and the head of Hayward security. But then again, maybe Haskell had considered this possibility and dismissed it because it was such a long shot. There was a lot I did not know about the PI game, and perhaps there was good reason to consider my little trip to be a waste of time.

Teddy and I went out as Bill began explaining to Rhonda just where he wanted to go next.

Although I was told to take Teddy with me, as in, in my car, that turned out to be impossible because he did not fit comfortably in it. Instead, Teddy drove me to Sun Provident's local offices in the big dark pickup truck that had been parked outside my house when Bill and I arrived an hour earlier.

At first it seemed unlikely that Harvey would cooperate with me, considering I had punched a hole in one of his tires, so I asked Teddy to stay outside when I walked up the wooden ramp to the trailer's rickety door. I poked my head in to see what kind of reception I would get, and Harvey spoke right up from his desk.

"Well, I guess I gotta look around my car now, don't I? Or did you come up with something better, like putting sugar in my gas tank this time?"

I didn't answer, instead leaning back out and saying Teddy's name softly. He understood immediately, hitching up his jeans and lumbering into the office behind me. I swear the floorboards made a cracking sound when he came inside.

"Hey, hey, hey! There's no need for any rough stuff here!" Harvey was up on his feet a moment later, his pudgy hands out in front of him and all semblance of hostility gone. There really is a value to bringing a superbig guy with you in some parts of this work.

"Relax, Harv. Siddown." I played it like an organized-crime guy, stepping up and dropping into one of the cheap chairs in front of Harvey's desk. Although I didn't look to see, I was reasonably sure that Teddy was staring at Harvey with a fair amount of malevolence.

"Look, that thing with the Gonzalez kid is outta my hands now. That Escobar guy has got half the lawyers in the Panhandle on it."

"Very good, Harv. You're brighter than you look. I thought I was going to have to explain this to you, and here you figure it all out yourself."

"What?"

"Escobar. Remember the day you dropped his name to me? The day someone leaned a nail up against your car tire? The day that Barstow sat right where I'm sitting?"

"Yeah." Harvey's worried face took on a look of suspicion at this point, as if he'd given away a secret that was going to get him into a lot of trouble but wasn't quite sure.

"Well, when I left to go over and see Escobar, someone called a couple of guys who tailed me from Escobar's law offices. And I bet our good buddy Bob made that phone call, and that he made it right from here."

He blinked at me a couple of times, looked back at Teddy, and then nodded.

"Yeah. Yeah, he did. You want the number?"

"Sharp as a tack, Harv." I turned and smiled at Teddy while Harvey began running nervous fingers through a stack of bills he picked up from a wooden in box near the phone. The billing cycle should have already come around by then, and even if it hadn't, I knew Sun Provident was as tightfisted with its employees as it was with its clients. Harvey was required to keep track of outside use of the phone, and it was a reasonable assumption to think he'd have the number somewhere.

It turned out to be a bad assumption, though, as he quickly showed me that the phone bill had not yet arrived and then protested that he had not written down the number Barstow had used. I was ready for that one as well.

"Harvey, you know we can find out that number, right? But that it would take us a while to do that? Well, maybe you'd be a sport and call the phone company and get that information for us. How about that?"

He was trying very hard to come up with a dodge for that one when Teddy spoke up.

"Frank."

"Yes, Teddy."

"Barstow didn't make that call. Your friend here did."

Remember I mentioned the very real value of a guy who can read people? I'm not one of those guys, and I make a point of noting people who are. I added Teddy to that list even as Harvey dropped the stack of envelopes and swallowed. Hard.

CHAPTER NINE

You might think that that revelation closed the case, but it wasn't quite that simple. Stone had come by to see Harvey the day he got handed the Gonzalez insurance claim, and he had given Harvey a number to call if anybody really began digging into what had happened. I am quite sure that the police would have been very interested in why Marty Stone wanted to know who was investigating the Gonzalez accident, but as evidence it didn't amount to much. I am quite sure that Stone was prepared to show that the accident had elevated his well-known concern with the jogging trail that his CEO used every night.

Harvey spilled everything right then and there, which was a help, but Teddy explained to me as we drove away that this was really a case of Harvey's word against Stone's. I got a mental image of Harvey sweating on the witness stand and I began to get that feeling of disappointment that had permeated so much of this case.

Even so, it was a big find and clearly indicated that Stone was very much involved in the accident. The bullet left on my kitchen table had been intended to run me off, so he was certainly trying to cover up whatever had happened that night. If Charlie, the Subaru night watchman could pick Stone's photo out of a stack of similar pictures, we would have further proof that he had been involved in the planning as well. However, it was already early evening when we left Harvey's trailer, and I was not sure that Lester would appreciate my bothering Charlie after hours. I decided to wait until the next morning to go see him.

Teddy had called Haskell on the cell phone and simply told him we needed to talk. He explained that Haskell was always concerned about electronic interception of their cell phone conversations and so they kept the discussions brief. Although the large PI scoffed at the idea that anyone was interested in what he and his boss had to say to each other, he did admit that in this case it was not a good idea to underestimate a professional security outfit working for multimillionaires.

Haskell was waiting outside my house when we got there. Rhonda was not in evidence, but Haskell was still wearing the look of frustrated concern I had seen when we parted company hours before.

"I have Rhonda digging into Stone's time as a cop." he said as we went through the front door and got the light on. "She's focusing on anybody that Stone might turn to in a pinch—informants, other PIs. Hopefully we can get some pictures and you might see the guy who was tailing you."

"Makes sense. Why do you look so worried?"

"Because Stone kept Spector from going jogging on the night he was supposedly trying to kill him."

I sat down slowly on the coffee table, unable to summon the brain cells to find a chair.

"He did what?"

"He kept Spector at work late on the night that Eddie Gonzalez was hit by the SUV."

"Why didn't Spector say that when you talked to him?"

"He doesn't know it. I called him right after you left, and Spector still thinks he was kept at the office that night tying up some loose ends on the sale of the company. When you kept harping on the idea that Stone wasn't the type to kill his own CEO, it put a bee in my head."

He crossed to the sofa and sat down facing me. "If Stone really meant to run him over on the jogging trail, which everything we've learned suggests is the case, then why wouldn't he know Spector was still at work? He cased the SUV a week before the job, he left nothing to chance in the hit-and-run itself, and yet he didn't know his own boss was stuck at the office." Bill tapped the wood of the coffee table with the tips of stiffened fingers as he said the last words.

"No. That doesn't make sense. So Rhonda and I went back out to Hayward and took Denise out for a coffee. She remembers it was a pretty crazy night anyway, all sorts of last-minute stuff, and a ton of people calling to protest the sale, but she remembers Stone telling her not to let Spector leave until he had the extra security guys there to go with him. As it turned out, Denise used the extra time to get Spector's customs stuff together and go over his itinerary with him, but the extra guards didn't get there until well after dark.

"Stone kept him from going jogging that night. Now if anybody can tell me why he got this thing in motion and then kept the victim out of the way, I'm all ears."

"He decided to call it off at the last minute?" I offered, thinking out loud.

"Come on. You met him. Does he look like the kind of guy who loses his nerve?"

"No." Stone looked like the kind of guy who could disarm a bomb while the building was burning down around him. "So he planned this thing, picked out the SUV, babysat it a couple of nights, scouted out a spot to hit Spector and another spot to dump the truck, and then tried to keep me from looking into the death of the guy they accidentally killed. Makes no sense."

"You guys are forgetting the psycho car thief kid," Teddy said from inside the kitchen. "Stone wasn't working alone. Maybe Stone was afraid the kid would mess it up and get caught. So he kept Spector out of the line of fire just because he figured it wasn't worth going to jail over a dumb mistake like this kid was sure to make. And the kid sure did make a mistake, didn't he?"

Haskell nodded, considering.

"Maybe. And maybe the kid wasn't involved at all. Maybe somebody else drove the truck, somebody really criminal, somebody from Stone's days as a cop. And something made Stone cancel the plan at the last minute, like he suspected his old friends could put him in a cell."

"Or maybe something happened during that last day that convinced him the merger was going to go through even if they pulled this off." I was thinking out loud again.

Haskell stood up and stretched, his back popping loudly under the dress shirt.

"Okay, let's stop guessing and go with what we can prove. Frank, tomorrow you and Teddy go see this Charlie and show him a picture of Stone. Between that and Harvey, we've got just enough information to get in deep trouble with the law if they ever take an interest in this case again. And who knows? We may have to turn this over to the cops just so someone can get Stone in a room and ask him just what the heck happened."

The next morning we went to Lester's Subaru dealership with the intention of finding out where Charlie worked in the courthouse, but Charlie was still there even though it was after nine. Lester met us at the door, and he was not pleased to see me.

"Well, thanks a lot, Mr. Cole. Here I thought we were helping you and it seems you decided to blab all over creation about what Charlie saw that night." His face was taut and he looked about ready to cry. Charlie was seated at one of the dealer desks in the main showroom, looking much more chipper than Lester.

"Lester, what happened?"

"What happened? What happened? Somebody came by last night and gave poor Charlie quite a scare, that's what happened. Lucky he's such a big guy . . . but now you tell me, who'd you go talking to about this?"

It fell into place quickly enough. My picture viewing at Hayward the previous day had been meant to rattle a few cages, but we'd forgotten that the other side knew about Charlie. After all, whoever had been casing the SUV had spoken with Charlie when he'd gone outside to watch the fire engines, and we had somehow overlooked that. I pushed past Lester and walked toward the big man at the desk.

Charlie was dressed for work, clad in his mechanic's overalls with the "Charlie" patch sewn on the chest and wearing the shined shoes with the white socks. He looked up at me with a face that was a mix of shame, uncertainty, and pride that left me completely flummoxed. He didn't wait for me to speak.

"Hi, Frank," he said in a low singsong, like a small child trying to gauge how much trouble he was in.

"Hi, Charlie. Lester said you had some excitement here last night."

"Who's your new friend, Frank?" Charlie was craning his neck over my shoulder in Teddy's direction. "He's big."

"That's my friend Teddy, Charlie."

"Frank, have you found your other friend yet?"

"No, Charlie, but we have a picture of him we'd like to show you. To make sure the man you saw that night is my friend." I was getting distinctly uncomfortable with referring to Stone in this way, mostly because there was a good chance that the affable security man was a murderer. In addition to that, there was an outside possibility that Charlie might end up testifying in court, and I could not imagine what a jury might make of Charlie's referring to Stone as "Frank's friend."

"You need to find him right away, Frank. There was a bad man here last night and I think he was looking for your friend, too."

"Tell me about the bad man, Charlie," I said, in a voice that was tight with anger. Until that moment I had not felt hostility toward the people who had killed Eddie Gonzalez and driven me from my home, but the very idea that they had bothered this man forced bile up into the lower part of my throat.

"He was almost as big as your friend over there, but thinner." Teddy heard the comment and frowned, conscious that his size could be mistaken for fat. "And his hair was yellow."

"What did he want?"

"He knocked on the door and I opened it. He asked me if I had seen you, Frank. And when I said yes, he asked if I had told you about your friend in the car."

Bingo. They had been hoping no one would find Charlie, but when I began reviewing the photographic archives at Hayward it could only mean that we had.

"Go on, Charlie. You're safe here."

"I know I'm safe here, Frank," he stated earnestly, as if my statement were so obvious as to be completely unnecessary. "He asked me if I had told you about seeing your friend, and I said I had. And he tried to tell me that I didn't, but I kept telling him that I did."

"What did he do then, Charlie?"

He looked down for a moment, but when he looked up again his eyes were growing animated.

"He *pushed* me, Frank. I was holding the door so he couldn't get in—"

"Charlie's not supposed to let anybody in. He's a good night watchman," Lester intoned from behind me, as if reciting a hymn.

"I'll bet you are, Charlie. What happened then?"

He looked over my shoulder and I believe that Lester gave some signal telling him it was all right to answer. Looking back to me, Charlie was unable to conceal his pleasure when he spoke.

"I *punched* him, Frank!" He brought a massive hand up to my left cheekbone and touched me with all the force of a gnat landing. "Right there!"

It was hard not to laugh, just from considering the fair degree of surprise that the midnight visitor must have experienced. Not to mention the pain. Charlie smiled broadly, looking over my shoulder, and when I looked I saw the same helpless mirth on the faces of both Teddy and Lester.

"What did the man do then?"

"He *ran,* Frank! He ran away!"

I pulled one of the printouts of Martin Stone from my jacket pocket and unfolded it while Charlie was still beaming. He looked down at the face and suddenly became quite serious.

"That's your friend, Frank. That's the man in the car."

Teddy and I asked Charlie a few more questions about what the blond visitor had looked like, and he sounded a lot like the man I had briefly seen on the highway outside of town a few days before. The connection with Stone was obvious, and the odds were highly in favor of this man and his buddy having placed a bullet on my kitchen table one day.

Lester pulled Teddy and me aside after a while, a little less agitated but clearly unhappy about something.

"Listen, I'm gonna take Charlie to the courthouse now, but there is no way in heaven he's gonna stay quiet about this. Judge Harris is going to know about this by noontime."

At the mention of Judge Harris, Teddy gave off a slight peep of what I had to think was alarm, and I looked at him questioningly.

"That's not good." He stated with a dry throat, "He's Florida's answer to Roy Bean."

"That's him." Lester smiled as if surprised that Teddy knew this. "He's got a black-and-white photo of Roy Bean's courthouse on the wall in his chambers. What's the sign in that picture? 'Only law east of the Pecos' or something like that?"

"Law west of the Pecos," Teddy answered, still looking cowed. When he saw that my inquisitive expression had intensified, he explained: "Bill and I got to stand at attention in those chambers about a year ago. I stared at that picture while Bill did the talking."

"So you're saying we've got a bit of a time crunch now."

"We need to get Bill on the phone right now. And you might be flying solo again for a while."

"Naw, naw, it was all a question of expectation of privacy." Bill's voice came across the phone. "I thought we were on very solid ground to be videotaping where we were, but Judge Harris saw it differently. Didn't do anything to us, mind you, the law's real squishy on that topic, but believe me it would not be good for Ted or me to show up in that courtroom again. Not for a while anyway."

Teddy had already pulled up stakes and headed back to Tallahassee. It all seemed like a lot of fuss when you considered that Teddy was nothing more than an interested third party, but he seemed to think that the police in Harris's jurisdiction would be coming for me by midafternoon and had no intention of standing next to me when that occurred.

"Bill, where are you?"

"Where do you think? I'm in my car headed back to Tallahassee. Listen, when that crazy judge sends for you, it's gonna be a lot better for you if you don't mention Haskell Investigations."

"Sends for me? Sends for me? Because a handyman got leaned on and reacted accordingly? I think all the justice we're ever gonna need got handed out when Charlie punched that guy. Who, by the way, is probably sporting quite a shiner by now."

"You don't know this judge, Frank. He doesn't have that Roy Bean picture on his wall for nothing. He wants people to think he's crazy."

"No, no, no, I've already got one crazy judge in my life and I don't need another." I could only imagine how Mark would react in his law office up north if he heard I'd run afoul of another magistrate. "We didn't do anything wrong, so you turn that car around, or you call this Judge Harris, and get this thing smoothed over. I thought that was your gig, anyway."

"It is, Frank, it is. And I keep all the friendly folks friendly by staying away from the ones who are unfriendly. These people all know each other, the politicians, the lawyers, the judges, and I am not taking any more chances with Harris. In the meantime, relax; you were doing some insurance investigating, you asked a few questions, and you have no idea how they got back to Charlie."

"That's not gonna wash."

"And it's not like we're off the case, Frank. Rhonda is still working Stone's known associates, she's coming up with some good leads there, and the judge doesn't know her, so she's still with you. Ted and I are gonna go back to the office and see if we can't switch one of our cases around to get someone else down there." As disquieting as this all was, it made some kind of sense when I remembered that he was working for Spector and that I was really just an ancillary concern.

"Whatever you do, don't mention the firm." I am not sure if he turned off his cell phone then, or if he finally got enough miles between us, but the line went dead at that point.

I hung up the phone and walked slowly into my living room. Remembering the blank check that Spector had handed Haskell, I had to believe that a disagreeable local judge was not going to knock the firm out of the game here. Unfortunately, I was equally sure that I was about to gain some more legal taint from yet another lunatic in a black robe and that all my careful efforts to rehabilitate my career were going to be ruined.

Thinking of the legendary Judge Harris reminded me of my own personal tyrant in the bankruptcy court up north. As I had explained to Gray Toliver so many days before, my judge had seemed asleep through half of the proceedings and had appeared to be nothing but an advertisement for mandatory retirement. He sure woke up at the end, though, and I swear it was the news of the completely unrelated corporate fraud case that had shaken him from his doldrums. Like the aforementioned Roy Bean, he had seemed to rise from a drunken stupor and proceeded to rail away at me as if I were the source of all the evils in corporate America. The memory still made my blood boil.

Well, that's not really true. It made my blood boil now, but when it happened I was still so far down in the dumps about losing the company that the full ramifications and the total injustice of his ruling didn't really register. I hadn't experienced this kind of blind resentment in the entire nine months I had been in Exile.

Maybe Charlie's visitor had done it to me. I remembered getting the first stirrings of a deep anger when the simple giant had told me how the other man had tried to frighten him, and only the revelation that Charlie had bested his visitor had eased that hot feeling.

Charlie's visitor. The same guy who had tailed me when Harvey had placed a phone call. A man sporting a shiner now.

I slowly pulled out the notepad I'd been carrying when Ted and I spoke with Harvey, and then I was out the door.

I actually did get to meet Judge Harris later that day, but not because anyone sent for me.

My first stop was back at the Exile town library, where I took up my customary seat in front of the computer. When I had done the first background checking on Hayward Shipping I'd had very little idea what to look for, but after the events of the last few days I had at least one good hunch. It turned out to be pure gold, as far as fact-checking goes, and before long I was asking Mary Beth Marquadt to see if I could use her office to make a call. I spoke briefly with Spector's assistant, Denise, at Hayward Shipping, and then I was back on the road.

I guess Judge Harris hadn't sent anyone to find me just yet, as I got to Hayward without any brushes with the law. Denise had gotten me cleared onto the docks, and the Hayward guards at reception waved me through with a smile. I took the stairs two at a time and was practically at a dead run when I went past Hurst's disciple, Natalie. She jumped up to stop me, got hung up trying to get out of the circular hallway cubicle, and didn't manage to catch me until I was inside Hurst's office.

The old man looked up from his desk with a face of total repose. I think he was actually expecting me, but when I smiled at him, it didn't fit his mental picture of how this was supposed to go, and he frowned slightly. Natalie spoke.

"I'm sorry, Mr. Hurst, he went right by me, I have no idea what he's doing here or how he got in! I'll call security right now."

"Oh, don't bother, Natalie. It's all right. I'm sure that whatever Frank has to say here is more important than the restructuring of the company anyway." He waved two spindly arms over a pile of papers and diagrams on his desk, and I could see that I had interrupted

Sanford Hurst while he was reshaping the world in his own image. I took a step forward.

"Looks like you already made some friends in Caracas," I observed, nodding at the papers.

"That will be all, Natalie." He said it pleasantly enough, but he now knew why I was there and sure didn't want me propounding my new-found wisdom in front of anybody. Natalie withdrew with a dire comment about being just outside the door, and I helped her attitude by suggesting she get me some coffee instead. The door slammed with an explosive crash.

"Please don't bait my staff, Frank."

I walked across the golden carpet and sat down without being asked. Hurst was impeccably dressed, as always, with a crisp white shirt and gold tie. His suit jacket was hung up near the door, and the rest of his office looked like Spector's across the hall. A few more diplomas, for sure, and a few pictures of horses running around a track, but otherwise the same.

"I guess congratulations are in order, huh?" I motioned again at the papers. "You're probably halfway to convincing the new owners that they can't get by without you."

"No need, Frank. Our CEO has deserted us and someone has to mind the store."

"You know, for the guy who found Spector you sure do talk bad about him."

"It's no secret that I have found Drew to be a total disappointment. And his underhanded betrayal of this company was completely out of line with how he represented himself during the vetting process. Even now I've got our corporate counsel's office reviewing his recruitment to see just how he could have misled us."

"That's good. He did exactly what you wanted him to do, and you're going to fire him for it."

"I've no idea what you mean." He was positively leering at me. I guess that's the problem with a really good scam like the one he'd run on his shareholders. If it works perfectly, nobody knows how smart you are. But now someone had figured it out, and he was so happy.

"Sure you do. It took me a little digging, but I finally found what I was looking for. The whole time I've been looking at Spector's involvement with Hayward Shipping I've been wondering why a turnaround expert gets recruited to run a completely healthy company."

"He wanted a challenge."

"No, he didn't. He saw that he was going to be allowed to rewrite the board's rules and pack it with his own people, and he came down here to make a fast buck and leave town. And that's exactly what you wanted him to do. You and the original board."

"I'm afraid I'm going to have to deny that, Frank." He seemed to be speaking for the benefit of unseen ears, or maybe a tape recorder.

"I'm not wired. But it makes no difference anyway. You see, most people around here don't understand just how badly you wanted to sell this company. They look at you and the original board and see a bunch of guys with everything going their way. And it was, except for one thing: The stockholders were getting more and more restive. Here you were, the president of a board of yes-men, and those pesky stockholders kept giving you grief. Talking about corporate governance and ecological awareness."

"It is amazing how people who don't know the first thing about the shipping business think they can dictate things like that." He was still amused.

"It sure is. And I wouldn't have discovered this animosity, except for the way you handled Spector's big betrayal. You screamed his name from the rooftops but never once mentioned which board member among your old cronies switched sides."

"I have no idea, it was a secret—"

"Save it for the press. You didn't savage whoever cast that fourth ballot because you put him up to it. In fact, it could have been any of the others because you were all in on it. You hated having to answer to an increasingly vocal gang of shareholders, and you used Spector to get out of it."

"Well, it is true that the stockholders will have to address their concerns to the competent people in Caracas." The smirk was back. I had no idea whether the laws of incorporation were any different in Venezuela, but even if they weren't, the Hayward stockholders were going to be just one group among many. Add in a foreign language and a whole lot of saltwater, and the likelihood that their concerns would be addressed or even heard went down a lot.

"So Spector comes down here, sells the company, and takes all the heat for something that was your idea all along."

"There is absolutely no evidence to support that."

"You're right. There's some minor stuff, like a rumor about a leveraged buyout by the original board—"

"Just a rumor."

"—that never materialized. And then there was a share buyback initiative that got defeated at the annual meeting—"

"It was a sound effort to repurchase outstanding company shares and prevent further dilution of the stock."

"And it would also have reduced the number of annoying people you had to listen to. In fact, if you'd been able to buy back enough of those shares and hand them out among yourselves as options, you might have had enough votes to ignore the other shareholders completely."

"Wonderful conjecture, Frank."

"Well, it doesn't matter anyway, does it? After all, I'm only here trying to figure out why a poor college kid got run over on a jogging trail a few weeks ago."

"Really? From the amount of effort you're putting into rumormongering, I would have thought you were starting your own tabloid."

I stood up, exhaling loudly as I rose.

"Tell me one thing, though. Right now I've got enough evidence to get your chief security guy dragged in for questioning in the attempted murder of Drew Spector. Now, if you were opposed to Spector's decision to sell the company, as you say you were, I'd consider you a prime suspect. You and the members of the original board. And going by what you said today and what you've said in the papers, it sounds like you had a lot of reason to hate that man.

"But if in reality you tricked him, if you actually wanted him to sell the company, then there'd be no motive for you to kill him. After all, he did what you wanted." I smiled as his face took on a minor expression of concern. "Now ain't that a shame? Either you hated him like you said in the papers, in which case you're a prime suspect, or you tricked him into selling the company, in which case you'd be in the clear. If only you could say so."

I started for the door slowly, enjoying the silence behind me. I didn't even turn to look as I put my hand on the knob.

"Either way, you're gonna end up answering some tough questions about the exact nature of your relationship to Mr. Drew Spector. And I sure hope you've worked this out with those four yes-men of yours."

I really don't know just how much of that summation was legally accurate, but it was designed to spook Mr. Hurst and it worked. I really needed to see the two guys who had tailed me, particularly the one with the black eye, and something told me Hurst wasn't going to just let me drive away.

When I finally saw that I had picked up my tail again, it made me wonder if they hadn't been watching me all along. The last time I had been aware of them had been that time on the forested highway between Davis and Bending Palms, and even Ted and Rhonda had believed my home was not under surveillance anymore. Even so, they slipped in behind me with such ease that I had to suspect they had been there for some time before I actually spotted them.

I had been checking the rearview mirror with great regularity, and even though it was a bright sunny Panhandle day there were not so many cars out and about that I couldn't see who was back there. Granted they were now driving an eggshell blue sedan, and the big blond man was wearing a large pair of sunglasses, but I should have noticed them when they picked me up, and I can't honestly say where that happened.

Anyway, they were three cars back on the highway outside Davis and two cars back as we got into Bending Palms. My nerves had been flaring with adrenaline and resentment when I left Hurst's office, but the intervening miles had drained that. I knew I was going to have to do something a little extreme, and to combat my failing nerve I took out one last bit of insurance.

The previous afternoon, Ted and I had convinced Harvey Webster to give us the number he had used to call these men a few days before. We had compared it to the emergency number that Sandy junior had used to call Stone when he'd been arrested. We had hoped it would be the same number, forming another connection to the Hayward security chief. Although this had turned out not to be the case, I doubted the trail car's occupants had changed phones in the course of this assignment.

"It's what we call a work phone," Ted had told me at the time. "Cell phone with no caller ID signature, onetime use, throw it away when the job is done."

I had keyed the number Harvey had given us into my cell phone before heading out, and I waited until I was stopped at a light with a good view behind me before hitting the button. I made sure they didn't see me doing it, with the cell on the seat beside my thigh, and I prayed for a long light as I stared into the rearview.

The blond man with the sunglasses answered a cell phone as I watched.

I fought the temptation to pick up the phone and say something, and simply turned the phone off as the light turned green. The blond man took the phone away from his ear and looked at it before shutting its cover, so I knew I had the right phone and the right guys. With that last piece of insurance in place, I headed for the scene of my big finale. I already knew where the courthouse was located in Bending Palms, having frequently done fact-checking work there, and I drove in that direction as casually as I could. The unidentified middle car was still between us, and I could only hope its driver had business in Bending Palms.

He did. The courthouse stood atop a long, low hill with one of Bending Palms' main streets running right in front of it. The car between me and my shadows turned and tucked itself into a parking space just as we approached the judicial headquarters of a magistrate who liked to compare himself to the most famous judge of the Old West.

My followers slowed down a lot when their cover turned off, and the gap between us widened as they tried to look like they had no interest in me whatsoever. There was about thirty yards of distance between my car and the blue trail car when we passed the courthouse, and I ate that up in the space of just a few seconds. I loved my Honda, and secretly hoped that Haskell could buy me a new one, but I was sick and tired of all this running, and I stamped on the gas with all my might once I got it into reverse.

My back bumper smashed into their engine compartment. I hadn't been able to get the speed up all that high in the short distance, but I was looking for lots of sound and, boy, did I get it. You would have thought a freight train had fallen out of the sky with the boom I made in that collision. The last thing I saw before I turned to face forward and put my chin on my chest was the image of two large men raising their arms in front of their faces in expressions of abject horror.

My poor car. The impact reduced its overall length by about ten percent, accordioning the trunk almost into the backseat. Both rear wheels were locked up against crumpled metal, and a liquid with a distressing smell began to pool immediately underneath the wreck. In the meantime I wasn't feeling all that hot myself, having experienced the sick sensation that accompanies a paralyzed diaphragm or a good punch to the kidneys.

I hadn't cared much about whether or not my two friends were hurt, but if I'd been injured it would have been a real problem. These guys were not going to hang around to be identified, and I needed to create an even bigger scene to keep them from drifting away in what was sure to be a great amount of confusion. Jumping from my car with the cheap throwaway camera in hand, I began hollering as if a live badger were trying to dig its way out of my insides. Stumbling toward the other car (I was hurt worse than I thought), I began snapping picture after picture of the two other men, all the while shouting that they had rear-ended me, that everyone was a witness, and that I was going to sue.

Boy, were they cool. Their hood was crumpled upward, and their front bumper was jammed under my rear bumper, but the one with the sunglasses silently slipped out on the passenger side while the driver started the car. Wisps of smoke came from their engine as the blond man surveyed the intertwined bumpers and then simply hopped up onto the hood. He was a big guy all right, and had obviously dealt with car accidents before. He jumped in the air just once, and the bumpers separated.

The street was filling with people, office workers mostly, and a car had pulled up behind the blue one by then. I was still shouting and snapping, not understanding why the men in the car were acting as if no one was there at all, when the blond got down and climbed back into the car. The other man backed off just enough to swing the ruined vehicle into the oncoming lane, and it was apparent that they were simply going to leave.

Most courthouses are swarming with police and security at all hours, but for some odd reason this one was not. Quite a few lawyer types had come out of the building to stand staring on the steps, and many windows had opened so that the barristers could look out, but no police. It was hard to believe.

I did see a bailiff come out with the crowd, though. I think he was merely on a cigarette break, but his presence was good enough. He was a balding middle-aged guy in a gray shirt with epaulettes and a badge, but he did have a gun, and I really did not want my shadows to disappear. I stepped into the path the escaping car would have taken to get out of this little jam, hoping that their very natural desire to run me over would be overruled by the presence of so many witnesses.

"Officer! Officer! They're trying to get away!"

He stared at me as if I were trying to get him to pluck an airplane out of the sky. I guess traffic accidents really don't fall under a bailiff 's duties after all, but the blue car now began edging around the crumpled rear of my Honda. It was clear that I was going to simply be nudged out of the way.

"Officer! Officer! These are the guys who bothered Charlie last night!"

I don't know if he understood me at first, but I kept pointing frantically and shouting Charlie's name, and he eventually got the idea. He also saw that I was snapping picture after picture of him standing there with a butt in his mouth (or thought he did; I had run out of film long before) and finally he swung into action. In a blur he was standing next to me, with one hand roughly holding a fistful of my shirt and the other imperiously pointing at the guys in the car.

The street began to fill with more bailiffs, and somewhere in all that the big blond's sunglasses got knocked off. Charlie's estimate of where he had tagged this guy turned out to be a bit on the low side, as the entire outside orbit of his left eye was a swollen crosshatch of angry flesh. One of the bailiffs took a decided interest in that shiner.

"Been anywhere near a Subaru dealership in the last twenty-four hours, sir?" The cuffs were coming out now that they knew who he was, and the questioner was shaking him back and forth in a tight, jerking motion.

You gotta love small towns.

My cell phone rang as I sat on a bench outside Judge Harris's chambers. The bench was all right angles and made of a hardwood that was becoming more uncomfortable by the minute, but that was probably because my back was tightening up from the accident. It turns out that my instinctive chin-on-chest action just before the impact was exactly what the doctor would not have ordered, as it basically gave me whiplash. This is usually an injury you get when you are hit from behind unexpectedly, and being the moving force in this instance I should have been better prepared for the crash. The funny thing was just how many people on that street swore up and down that they had seen the blue car rear-end me, and I certainly did nothing to correct that.

Not that there was much opportunity for me to talk. Judge Harris had indeed heard of Charlie's late-night fisticuffs and been quite eager to meet me (both Tate and Dannon later admitted they had been instructed to find me immediately), but with the culprits in custody he had other people to grill.

And so I was sitting uncomfortably in one of the building's quiet side hallways when my cell phone rang. It was Rhonda.

"Frank, I've got some news!" She sounded excited, and I let her run.

"You know how we were looking at Stone's known associates from his days as a cop? Well, I think we were looking in the wrong place. I've been digging and digging and all I came up with was a whole bunch of people who used to work with Stone who say he was squeaky clean, that he would never have anything to do with anybody he ever busted."

I had to figure that such a policy would rob a cop of a good source of informants, but I let it go while I shifted around on the bench.

"So I got to thinking: We're looking for professionals, right? We just assumed he wouldn't use anybody from Hayward Security, but why wouldn't he? I mean, I'll bet they're loyal, and if one of the company bigwigs' sons is involved—"

"Rhonda, what did you find?"

"I asked around for a Hayward Security guy, an investigator type, who would fit your description of the guy who was tailing you. And I think I hit pay dirt, Frank. I've got some photos of this one guy, Stone's right-hand man, they tell me, he's big, he's blond—"

"And his name's Don Harper. Right?"

I wish there was a nicer way to tell her what I had learned about my tails while sitting in that hallway, but I didn't see one at the time, and my back was really giving me fits. I guess I ruined her big moment, because there was a long silence at the other end.

"How'd you know?" She waited only an instant before asking, "Has something new happened, Frank?"

Maybe it's an exaggeration to say I got to talk to Judge Harris, as it was only a brief handshake in the hall and boy was I relieved. The door to his chambers opened and he emerged, followed closely by what looked like three lawyers and a captain in the state police. Harris was the oldest, and clearly in charge, but he wasn't wearing the robe and appeared quite small in his light gray suit and wingtips.

A salt-and-pepper beard sat closely cropped on his face, but a mass of unruly graying hair burst outward just above his ears. He looked as if he were wearing a scouring pad. The men with him were all scratching notes or waiting to do so, and they almost blew right by me. I had been waiting to get chewed out and possibly tossed in jail for an evening, and I didn't make a move to get Roy Bean's attention.

He stopped suddenly and wheeled like a dancer. The others parted so he could see me.

"There you are." He glowered at me with magisterial wrath and I was transported back in time to a bankruptcy court in a colder climate. His voice was deep for such a small guy. "Stand up, boy, when I talk to you."

I got to my feet with difficulty, and he stepped in quickly, taking my hand.

"Good job, boy. Outstanding." He was close enough for me to smell his breath, and the eyes under that mop were bright and alive. The accent was pure Louisiana, though not Cajun. "I called that smooth-talking snake-oil salesman Haskell, and by goodness we're gonna have a murder indictment before the night's out. Maybe even pull that Sanford Bouillabaisse Hurst the Third into court just for the fun of it."

He suddenly became aware of my twisted posture and called back through the now-open door leading into his offices. A bailiff scampered out.

"Bob, Mr. Cole here needs to get to the hospital. Whistle up an ambulance, and tell Doc Severn to take special care of him." He turned back to me. "How's that sound?"

"Thank you, Your Honor. They told me you were kind of a Roy Bean judge and I was a little worried about the reception I was going to get."

He leaned in again, and the voice dropped considerably.

"There's almost no evidence that Bean ever hanged anybody at all. He was a fast-talking self-promoter like your friend Haskell there." He pulled back and announced for the crowd, "Besides, old Judge Bean never hanged a man who did him a favor. Let's go."

The group moved off like a gulf hurricane.

Later that night, after I got to talk with Mark in New York, I was in a hospital bed for observation. Though only thirty, I was starting to learn that older bodies do not bounce back from minor injuries the way young bodies do. In the meantime Mark was of two minds regarding what I told him.

"Uh, Frank, I'd like to say how proud I am that you stayed on the case and worked it out for this Escobar family."

"It was more for the Gonzalez family, actually. Mike Escobar has done more harm than good here."

"Lawyers, huh?" We both laughed. "Well, it's all good as far as something we can point to about what a good guy you are and how you've been spending your time down there. Make sure you keep in touch with all of these people, Escobar, Gonzalez, anybody who would say something nice about you.

"But in the meantime, buddy, you have *got* to be more careful around the law down there!" He was laughing helplessly, but he obviously felt that his entire strategy for rehabilitating my corporate life was in serious jeopardy. "I mean, we talked about this before you even went down there. You were just supposed to do some simple background stuff—"

"They put a bullet on my kitchen table."

"Exactly. You should have dropped this one right then and there. Remember, this is just a sideline, something to show you're employed but not making anywhere near enough to start paying off any settlement . . . Wow, they actually put a bullet on your kitchen table?" I had already told him about that, but I guess he lost sight of it in all the other minutiae. His voice lost its exasperated tone, which suggested that he was starting to understand my motivation to see this particular investigation through to the end. There's a reason he graduated at the top of his law school class.

"And then they used my background check to justify denial of the claim. Not to mention trashing out the reputation of a dead guy."

"Okay, tiger." Normally I didn't care for that appellation, and I also didn't care for the way that Mark treated me like a life that was in receivership, but somehow his words didn't carry the weight they once had. Maybe it was because there was no way that Mark Ruben would ever back a car into anybody. Come to think of it, there was no way I would have done that three years ago. Even nine months ago.

"So the doctors said they'd let you out tomorrow?"

"It's just for observation. They gave me some happy pills and I'm gonna have to take it easy for a few days."

"Sunny Florida."

"Sunny Florida." I was drifting off at that point, so we said our good-byes. Just before signing off, though, Mark called my name one last time.

"Frank."

"Yeah, buddy."

"Great job. I'm proud of you."

Later, with the lights in the hospital room turned off but a yellow glow shining in from the corridor outside, a friendly voice came at me out of the darkness. Beth Ann's hand took mine and a set of invisible lips pressed gently against my forehead.

"Hey there, crazy man," she whispered, and I began to make out her shape in the gloom.

"What time is it?" I asked, looking about me in vain for a clock.

"After visiting hours, if that's what you mean. My cousin is a nurse here."

"Breaking hospital rules. You're gonna get me in trouble."

"Oh, I'd say you don't need my help for that. The whole town's talking about you. Crazy Yankee, driving your car through the front door of Judge Harris's courtroom."

"That's not what happened . . ."

"The story I heard, you were exchanging gunshots with a truckload of hired assassins."

"That would be a tough one. I don't know one end of a gun from the other."

"I'll teach you."

"I thought you were my photography teacher."

"So did I, until I saw those atrocious pictures you took with that cardboard camera. I had to tell people I didn't know you. I could lose my teaching posit—"

"They didn't."

"Oh yes, they did. Rushed that film right over to my shop. I haven't laughed like that in years."

We both giggled quietly in the dark, and when she kissed me again it wasn't on the forehead.

CHAPTER TEN

"So Stone disappeared and no one's seen him for days." I moved a pawn as I finished the story for an absolutely enraptured Gray Toliver. We were back at our customary spot at the Exile public beach, the sun was shining, and the chess game was a sideshow.

"You got him, Frank." Gray was beaming with pride. "I knew you would. When you left here that day I figured on not seeing you for a while, but I said to myself, 'Frank's really got his teeth in this one, and I wouldn't want to be the other guys.' "

"Well, we're not quite out of the woods yet. The two guys from the car didn't say a word, and in an hour that courthouse was filled with lawyers from Hayward and then a bigger bunch hired by the Hurst family. So by keeping their mouths shut they were only up for stalking and trying to leave the scene of an accident."

"But this Charlie fellow hit one of them."

"Yeah, and that counts against the blond one, Harper. But all that comes down to is assault, trespass, maybe some kind of intimidation with a possible witness."

"Wait a minute. There's too many connected things here for that. Stone went to the insurance guy to arrange some kind of notice if someone went looking into Gonzalez's death. That alone is huge. Second, Stone's right-hand man tries to intimidate the night watchman who saw Stone casing the SUV that was used in the killing. Third, Stone's right-hand man was tailing you, the insurance investigator, when you had your accident. And then Stone simply disappears.

"Doesn't that all add up to something in the eyes of a prosecutor?"

I smiled at him fraternally. For a guy who hadn't gotten an update on the case in days, Gray certainly seemed to follow it well.

"You should go to law school, Gray. No kidding. You've got the mind for it. And you're right; they're trying to pull the pieces together, but without Stone it's pretty hard."

"But you must have accomplished what you set out to do." He looked at me with a sly expression, letting me know he hadn't got caught up in the nonsense. He moved a bishop and I had to concentrate.

"Right again. No matter what happens with the rest of this, the insurance claim filed by Anneliese Escobar has been paid in full."

"Rosie must be happy. It wasn't right that he lost his son and then watched the poor kid's name getting dragged through the mud."

"I've got free automotive for life, so I guess he *is* happy." I moved my queen just because I didn't have any choice and watched Gray put my king in check. "And that's good, because the Honda's in tough shape."

"How about you? How's the back?" The night in the hospital had done me a world of good even though my back was still sore days later. The doctors told me I'd given myself a good wrenching, but as with most back and neck injuries only time would tell.

"Feeling good now that the case is over. I've been taking it easy, lying in the sun, you know, just enjoying the Florida life."

"And your girlfriend?" He checkmated me, but I wasn't paying attention.

"She's not my girlfriend. Yet. But, yeah, she got a few laughs out of that ridiculous roll of film I shot outside the courthouse. Good thing they didn't need any of those shots to identify these guys." I began setting up my pieces again. "We're going to dinner tonight."

"Outstanding." Gray's face turned into a slight squint as he looked over my shoulder, and in a dull tone he asked, "Frank, is this Stone a great big guy with dark hair?"

I turned quickly, feeling a jolt of pain down my spinal column, just in time to see Stone hold up both hands from a spot out on the sand. There were some people on the beach behind him even though it was early, and he had walked up to within ten yards before Gray spotted him. His hands were empty, even though he could have been concealing something under the big short-sleeved shirt, which he wore untucked over a set of khakis.

"Please don't be alarmed, Frank," he said evenly, his hands still up and open. "Chief Dannon is going to be here in just a few minutes and I wanted to talk to you first."

"All right," I said, feeling pretty unsure of all this but figuring he could have just walked up and hurt me without going through any of the ceremonial stuff.

"Can we speak privately?"

"Not a chance, buster." Gray's voice boomed behind me, and I actually started with surprise. "He's not going anywhere."

"I meant right here. But I want to talk to Frank alone."

If this was an attempt on my life it was sure an elaborate one. And in the meantime I'd meant what I'd said to Gray: There were far too many loose ends in this case and I desperately wanted to know what had actually happened. Looking at the big man standing there with his hands showing, I have to admit I still didn't believe he did it.

"It'll be all right, Gray. We won't go far." I got up, seeing Gray's chief petty officer face for the first time. He was glaring at Stone with an expression that was designed only for the act of murder, and he didn't take his eyes off the big security man as I walked over. We stepped a few paces off of the cement area and Stone began.

"I called Chief Dannon a few minutes ago, and when he gets here I'm turning myself in."

"But you didn't do it."

He smiled helplessly, looking down at the sand, and for the briefest instant I saw what he must have looked like as a teen, just a football player with a good head on his shoulders.

"I figured you knew. And if you hadn't tried so hard to make things right for that Gonzalez kid I wouldn't have bothered coming by here. But you're right. I didn't do it.

"Which is not what I'm going to tell the police, but I wanted to tell somebody the truth."

"Did you tell Hurst?"

"Oh yeah. Right after it happened. Heck, somebody had to tell him what the kid had done."

"So it was the kid."

"Yep. Only it wasn't entirely his fault." His face grew dark. "Frank, you gotta understand that Sandy's dad never gave a hoot about him at all. I'm more his father than that guy ever was. And there's a lot to like about that kid, too, if that self-centered snob had ever taken the time to get to know him. I swear that's why the kid did it. He just wanted that old man's attention, just once.

"Anyway, the news that the company was being sold hit Hurst hard. He's one of those hard-charging business types, the company's had a Hurst on the board for generations, and he'd picked Spector personally. Between you and me I have no idea what anybody sees in that Spector; he's a pretty boy with a good press agent and no backbone. He's almost competent at selling companies off, but he's got no talent I could see when it came to actually running them.

"But that's beside the point. The old man went nuts when Spector decided to sell the company, and I guess he went on a rampage at home, yelling and screaming. Well Sandy has always wanted the old man's attention, and as you know he doesn't think inside the law, so he saw a chance to finally get his dad to notice him." He stopped for an instant. "Imagine that. The kid's got a first-rate mind, Frank, knows cars and engines like nobody's business, and look what he had to do to get a little face time with his own father."

"So he did it."

"I didn't know what he was up to until the day it was supposed to happen. When the merger was announced, things at the office got very busy. I was away for most of that time, arranging security in Caracas. What a nightmare. I don't speak the lingo, I've never handled anything that big before, and I'm gonna just tell you it ate up all my time.

"Anyway, the kid was distant when I came back. He was spending a lot of time away from home and screening his phone calls. I had left Harper in charge of looking out for him, but nobody's ever been able to reach the kid the way I have. So I figured the kid was avoiding me because he was mad that I had been gone so much.

"That was until I talked to Harper and a couple of other guys from the Hurst family detail. The kid had actually been talking to them a lot, asking real screwball questions. They thought he was just interested in the cases they'd seen in other jobs, but if they'd paid any attention they would have known he was putting the final touches on something."

"These were the guys who were supposed to keep him out of trouble?"

"I made a mistake. More than one. I should have found more time for him when I got back. And when I suspected he was arranging something worse than a car theft, I should have stopped him."

"You did stop him. You kept Spector late at work that night."

"I should have done more. I had my guys tail the kid after I came back from Caracas, and they said he'd been casing the jogging trail and a Subaru dealership in Bending Palms. It didn't take a genius to see why he was looking at the jogging trail, but I actually had to go out to the dealership to learn why he'd spent so much time watching the place. That's when that Charlie guy spotted me."

He stopped for an instant, looking across the parking lot as if seeing Dannon's car. Apparently that was not the case, though, and I guess he was still chewing over his role in what had happened.

"I didn't want to tell Spector my theory, and the guy wasn't getting out on the fitness trail too much during the merger anyway. I put extra security on Spector, and before long it was the last night he'd be in country before the big signing. I kept him late at the office just to be sure, and then I tried to call the kid. I left him a message saying I was on to him and that Spector wouldn't be out there.

"He didn't believe me, Frank. Or maybe he didn't want to believe me. He might have started with this plan to get in good with his dad, but somewhere along the way I think he got hooked on the idea of killing someone. He always went the wrong way when he was alone, and I was just gone too long.

"He called me back when it was done."

I didn't ask how the kid had reacted to the event, but judging from the cloudy face in front of me, he had not found it unrewarding.

I heard a car door slam behind me, and I looked over to see Denny Dannon walking quickly across the grass a good fifty yards away. He was in uniform, complete with the state trooper hat and shades, and his hand was on his gun. Seeing me there, Dannon was clearly concerned that Stone had invited him to witness a murder-suicide, but he slowed down when Stone showed him his hands.

"So why are you taking the fall here?" I asked, speaking quickly.

"Because I never should have tried to cover it up. I thought I could control this, and look what happened. I got two of my own guys in hot water with the law. Do you know that they're accessories to a murder right now? I can straighten that out, but I have to turn myself in to do it."

"Don't. Don't do it. Not this way. Get Hurst's lawyers in here! You can get your guys off the hook without going to jail for the rest of your life!"

"Don't get it, do you? I never should have involved them in the first place. I was their *boss*."

Dannon came up then, looking worried, but Stone already had his hands behind his head and was telling the chief that he would go quietly. They spoke cop talk for a moment, and then he was in handcuffs.

CHAPTER ELEVEN

Sunday mornings I go to church and then get a big coffee at Exile's only sidewalk cafe. It's actually just a couple of tables set up outside the diner, but I take the Sunday paper and just unwind, watching people go by and catching up on the headlines.

"Morning, Frank." It was Dannon, dressed in a brown sport coat, tan slacks, and a red shirt open at the neck. He was one of those guys who would look cool wearing a clown suit. "Mind if I sit down?"

"Not at all. Paper?" I offered him the pick of the sections but he shook his head as he pried the lid off of the coffee he'd bought in the diner behind us. As I had not seen him inside, I had to presume he had been waiting to talk to me. I gently pushed the front page away from me so he could speak.

"That was a very nice thing you did for the Escobars and the Gonzalez family. Especially after your police chief didn't even try to help you."

"Sure you did. You told me Eddie was clean. And he was. Twice you had to tell me."

"Well, you're not the brightest guy I ever met, Frank."

We were smiling in the middle of that when a very large Town Car rolled into sight and stopped at the curb in front of us. One of the Hayward Shipping security guys stepped out from behind the wheel, and the one whom I had fingered as one of my tails got out on our side. He was smiling maliciously in my direction. I was suddenly happy that the chief of police was sitting beside me.

He opened the rear door, and Hurst got out in his Sunday best, an expensive blue double-breasted with a gold tie and a sky-blue shirt. He buttoned the jacket as he stepped up to the table, ignoring the chief and smiling at me.

"Good morning, Frank." He smiled a bit wider, and it became apparent he knew where to find me. "We were out for a drive and I happened to see you over here."

"Lucky me."

"Very lucky, Frank. Very." He looked up and down the street in distaste, a dandy tolerating the sticks for a moment. He stared at the glass windows of the diner and almost wrinkled his nose at what he saw inside. "I'd only heard about Exile until now. It's really very . . . quaint."

"Heard from Spector lately?"

"Oh, Drew's not with the company anymore, Frank. He tendered his resignation just a few days ago. Did quite well, what with the merger and the terms of his contract, but I don't think he was going to last anyway, not with the current management."

He was trying to make me think that he'd already fooled the new bosses from Caracas and that he'd somehow come out on top of all this. That was what he was doing here.

"You know, Mr. Hurst, you might want to check into my background a little bit. You'll find I had a pretty substantial company of my own, once."

"And lost it, too."

"That's right. But for a while there I ran with some people a lot like you. Money people."

"Are you threatening me? With these rich friends of yours?"

"No need. Spector's going to do that for me. What I was trying to say was, money people have their own way of getting even with each other. And Spector thinks he owes you big-time."

His smile flickered for an instant, but he regained his calm right away. I doubted this was news to him.

"I can't be held responsible for what people think."

"The guy who did my company's advertising said the same thing."

He actually blanched when he tried to get his arms around that one. It was not just out of the blue, but it was also so ridiculous that it offended him as a businessman. It probably would have killed him to know I was telling the truth, but all the same I didn't let him recover.

"How's little Sanford? Enjoying Europe?"

"Doing very well, thank you. Everyone should live abroad at least once in their lives."

"So what do you think he'll do when he gets home?"

"Excuse me?"

"He really liked old Stone, and he can't be too happy that the only man who ever cared about him is headed to jail." I smiled as if another humorous comment had occurred to me. "Hey. They drive on the wrong side of the street over there in Europe, don't they?"

"What?"

"I mean, who knows how good a driver he's going to be when he gets back? It takes a while to get used to driving on the right side of the road again, I imagine." I dropped the smile and said the rest in a flat tone. "And if I were you, mister, the moment that monster gets back to America I'd start looking both ways before crossing the street."

"I'm going to remember you, Frank."

Dannon had heard enough, and gently dropped his badge on the table.

"And I'm going to remember you said that, sir. Dennis Dannon, chief of police."

Hurst's handlers already had him by then, and they stuffed him back into the car's darkness with great efficiency before surging away. We both watched them disappear in the distance, and after a decent interval Dannon took a pair of reading glasses out of his jacket pocket and reached for the paper. As he sorted through it, looking for the section he wanted, he asked quietly:

"That true, Frank? You used to run with the rich people?"

"Don't be impressed. I married money."

"Wish I'd done that."

"It's overrated," I said.

He found what he was looking for and began reading.

On Monday I took a long bus ride to Tallahassee, enjoying the Florida landscape as it raced by the window. I took some time to walk around the city, too, feeling my injuries loosening up in the sun and in no hurry to be anywhere. After an hour or so I ended up near Bill Haskell's office, and so I headed in.

His office manager practically hissed at me when I came through the door, and I had to believe that it was something personal. After all, I had brought a ton of money to that firm, and office managers are usually very concerned about the books. Spector had paid off handsomely once the truth came out, and he had already been on the hook for every hour that Rhonda, Ted, and Bill worked on the case. More important, he was profoundly grateful that his uncomfortable employment situation had been so radically altered in his favor. Instead of being castigated as a villain who had sold the company, he was now quite the sympathetic character. And in the meantime the chief of security had admitted to attempting to kill him, so whatever severance package he was going to get had probably increased by a factor of ten.

Haskell was bubbling over, and in a flash I was seated in a comfortable chair in his office, drinking a very decent cup of coffee and shooting the breeze.

"And I wangled your car repairs into the company's insurance policy, Frank, so don't worry about that. Heck, it happened on the job, so of course you're covered."

This whole thing had started with an insurance claim, and the irony was not lost on me. Additionally, I did not want to get the money for the repairs from Haskell as part of my pay, fearing that this would brush up against my court-imposed income ceiling, so having the insurance cover it was perfect.

"Now, I do understand that you don't want your part of the payoff here, but I have to tell you it's substantial." No matter what else you could say about Haskell, you could not call him tight. "Maybe I should just set it aside, and you can draw against it when you need to. Kinda hush-hush."

"Thanks, Bill, that's very decent of you, but I really have to avoid even the appearance of trying to trick the court. Just one wrong step and my whole act is blown. Thanks anyway."

He nodded gravely, and took an envelope out of the desk.

"Well, there it is, then. The standard rate for a background check. You sure that's enough?"

"It goes pretty far if you manage it." I took the money and tucked it inside my jacket. I wasn't wearing a tie, and had brought the jacket just so I wouldn't look like a bum.

He smiled at me as we both rose, and we shook hands.

"So long, fact-checker. You might be hearing from me sooner than you think."

"You know where I am."

It was early the next Wednesday morning, and I was sitting with Gray at the chessboard as usual. In the distance two sailboats tacked lazily back and forth, and the gulls glided easily over the wind on the water. I had just finished telling him about the encounter with Hurst and his people, and there wasn't a line in that story that Gray didn't like.

"Yeah, that's our Chief Dannon for you. He's not afraid of anybody. I would have given a month's retirement check to have been there."

"Well, it made me feel a whole lot safer having him there, I can tell you that."

"Aw, they were just trying to rattle you, let you know they had your routine down. And that Hurst guy sounds like he really wanted you to think he's got his world back in order."

"He might. Guys like that have a habit of surviving. But Haskell did tell Spector about what I'd discovered."

"You mean your suspicion that they hired Spector knowing he'd sell the company?"

"Yeah. And according to Haskell, Spector wasn't happy at all. He's taken quite a beating in the business news over this, and you can bet Hurst was behind those stories as well. All sorts of speculation that he's a one-trick pony, that you should only hire him if you want to lose your business, that sort of thing."

"It's pretty much the truth, isn't it?"

"It sure seemed like it to me. But then again there's the truth that everybody knows and the truth that everybody says. In this case I think Spector didn't like having everybody say it."

"I am so glad I never went into the business world."

I let the conversation drift while I focused on the board. I was doing well in this match, even if I suspected Gray was a little preoccupied with my story. I made a move that was going to cause Gray some real problems, and he simply smiled at me. He didn't even look down at the board, and after it got to be too long I had to ask.

"What's the smile for?"

"It's your game, Frank," he said, still beaming. "It's improving."

O'Neil, Vincent H.

Murder in exile.

DATE			